The Bishop's Granddaughters

A Novel

This one's also for you, Ma.

Preface

This novel is one of a trilogy of novels written by the author that examine strong, interesting women at home, at work, at worship, and at play, including their love lives. Again you will see Rev. Viola Flowers up close as she bravely administers to her little flock in times of joy and sorrow, all while wrestling with the purity of her own faith. This time she learns something about her family that occurred years ago that is very shocking. "Sweet Jesus, was grandpa involved in those awful murders?" she moans to herself. Her grandfather was a legendary bishop in the Church of God & Spirit. Her father was also a prominent minister in that church. This is not a thriller or murder mystery. It's a novel about a courageous lady preacher whose religious faith must carry her through many serious challenges, including the possible disgrace of her family.

Chapter One

The Georgia moon shone down brightly on a small cabin nestled back in the pine trees. It had rained earlier in the evening, with lightening striking a nearby oak tree, splitting it in two. Out back by the woodpile a large copperhead snake slithered along the ground searching for rats. The eyes of a fat opossum looked out from the marsh grasses. Up the road from the cabin a hound dog howled when the moon began disappearing behind some black clouds that were about to bring more rain.

A man moved stealthily amid the tall pines and then emerged from the trees and stepped quietly upon the old dilapidated porch of the cabin. Bam! He violently kicked the door in, sending shards of wood across the room, and raised his double-barrowed shotgun and aimed at the naked couple in the bed. "Eeeeee!" the young woman in the bed screamed in the moonlight as she tried to cover up her nakedness. The man lying next to her sat bolt upright with terror-filled eyes. "Boom! Boom!" the shotgun rang out in the night when the man in the doorway fired both barrows. He reloaded it with shells from his coat pocket and walked over to the bed. Then he cold-bloodedly finished the job, this time nearly blasting the couple's heads off. He spat upon the woman's bloody body, then turned and vanished into the night.

Now the black clouds had totally enveloped the moon, leaving the Georgian countryside in even greater darkness. An owl hooted forlornly in the woods as a motor car chugged off sluggishly. The year was 1910.

****

"Whadda we have here, Leroy?" the fat-faced sheriff asked his young deputy who had arrived on the scene first. The two white men put handkerchiefs to their mouths and noses and entered the cabin and went over to the bed. The horrible stench and all the maggots left little doubt that the murder victims had been dead for weeks when their bodies were found by two teenage boys hunting in the woods.

"There's not much left of their faces, Chief. We're going to need fingerprints to identify these bodies," the deputy said grimly as he and the sheriff walked back out onto the porch to get some fresh air.

"This is Melvin Jenkins' place, but that dead nigger in there sure in hell ain't Melvin. He's much younger than Melvin," the deputy said as he began rolling himself a cigarette from a bag of Bull Durham he had pulled from his hip pocket.

"Put that tobacco away and go around back and look for Melvin's whiskey still. I know it's out there somewhere. I'll look around here." The sheriff grimaced as he put the handkerchief back to his face and reentered the cabin. Following orders, the deputy moved into the woods carefully looking for footprints. The copperhead snake looked on with pebble eyes from the woodpile.

****

Later that afternoon the sheriff arrested Melvin Jenkins, a Negro man somewhere in his thirties, who was well known in the area for bootlegging. Many people in the county believed Melvin Jenkins made the best liquor in that part of Georgia.

"Why are we arresting Melvin, Chief? We know he was locked up over in Benson County at the time of the murders, and couldn't have done it. And we didn't find any of his whiskey stills," the deputy said, thinking that Melvin's just owning the shack wasn't sufficient reason to arrest him.

The sheriff removed a tin of chewing tobacco from his desk drawer and packed a big pinch of snuff between his cheek and gums. "Don't you know anything, boy. How else are we gonna get that nigger to give us any information unless we keep his black ass behind bars for awhile," the big-bellied sheriff growled at his young deputy.

The young deputy rolled himself a cigarette. "I don't think he knows any more, Chief. He's told us that the man in the cabin was his cousin visiting from Memphis. He's still pretty shaken up about his cousin's death. I believe him when he says he doesn't know who the young woman is."

"Well I don't believe him. I think he knows her identity, and I'm gonna keep his skinny black ass locked up until he tells us," the sheriff snorted.

The deputy lit his cigarette. "She certainly wasn't from around here. Colored people around here couldn't afford the expensive clothes she was wearing. They must've been purchased in Atlanta," he said.

"Or stolen in Atlanta," the sheriff said as he got up from his desk. "Whoever she was, she was a pretty young thing. Even with her face half blown off, you could see that."

The sheriff spit and shot a wad of blackish gook that landed perfectly in the spittoon a few feet from his desk. He always got bull's-eyes. He wiped his chin with the back of his hairy hand and hitched his breeches and strolled back to the jail cell to talk some more with Melvin Jenkins.

He was determined there would be no unsolved murders in his county.

Chapter Two

It was late afternoon in Los Angeles in 1995. The parsonage sat behind some green hedges next door to the church. An attractive black woman in her early fifties, Rev. Viola Flowers was the pastor of the Church of God & Spirit. Her congregation bought the church and parsonage some years ago from a white church that moved to the San Fernando Valley after most of its parishioners moved there.

Rev. Flowers and her sister Lettie, her only sibling, were seated at Viola's kitchen table talking about the family reunion in Georgia that Lettie had returned from yesterday, where she enjoyed herself immensely. While in Georgia, by talking to different relatives, Lettie learned much about their genealogy that she hadn't known before, and had managed to fill in many blanks in their family tree.

"I must've gained ten pounds from all that good down-home cooking," Lettie grinned as she raised her blouse and showed her sister the large safety pin she needed to hold her skirt on because the button wouldn't reach the buttonhole. "I brought back Aunt Mildred's bread pudding recipe you wanted. Aunt Mildred said that for the lemon whiskey sauce any good whiskey will do."

She laughed, "Girl, I couldn't believe how old all our cousins have gotten."

"They're probably saying the same about you," Vi chuckled, "It's called aging. That's why I hate reunions."

Vi had just gotten out of a long contentious church committee meeting and was glad to be back in the quiet of her own kitchen, her favorite spot in the house. Because her feet were killing her, she had kicked off her shoes and was walking around in her stocking feet. She had an hour until her next appointment in her office next door at the church. It had been a very busy day for her, including performing a big wedding that morning.

Lettie reached into her handbag and handed Viola Flowers something wrapped in an old silk scarf. "Before I forget. Here. Aunt Jennie said to give you this. She said Aunt Belle wanted you to have it." Aunt Belle was their grandfather's sister.

"What is it?" Vi asked.

"The family Bible."

Viola carefully removed the old dog-eared Bible from its silk wrapping and flipped through it. "Who are the 'Bustersons'?" she asked Lettie, referring to the people listed in the family history section of the Bible. It was a surname she was unfamiliar with. There was even a Tom Busterson, a person with the same first name as their father and grandfather.

"I don't know," Lettie replied cavalierly, since she hadn't bothered to look at the old Bible.

Lettie reached over and helped herself to a cookie from the jar on the counter. She had just gotten off from work and was a little hungry. Unmarried with nobody at home waiting for her, she didn't know whether to go home and cook herself something, or stop for a bite at a restaurant on the way home.

With a puzzled brow Viola looked up from the old Bible. She had found no mention of the "Crombies," their family name. Only "Bustersons."

"Are you positive this is our family Bible?" she asked her sister skeptically.

"That's what Aunt Jennie said. She said Aunt Belle gave it to her before she died to give to you," Lettie answered as she munched her cookie.

Because Viola was the oldest, Lettie saw it as only natural that the family Bible be given to her. Aunt Jennie was from their mother's side of the family, while Aunt Belle, who was a couple of generations older than Aunt Jennie, was from their father's side of the family. Both sides of the family were originally from Georgia and were very close. Aunt Jennie still lived in Georgia and was the person who looked after their Aunt Belle until the latter went into a nursing home where she died.

"Some of the pages on our family history have been ripped out!" Vi said with alarm.

"Let me see." Lettie took the Bible and flipped through it and saw where some pages had been torn out, but she wasn't concerned about it. "There're a thousand possible explanations for those missing pages, Vi. There's also the possibility that because of her failing eyesight, Aunt Belle gave Aunt Jennie the wrong Bible by mistake. Who knows? You know how some old people are. They reach for one thing, while really wanting something else," she said unconcerned.

As an afterthought she said, "Maybe someone in the family got that Bible from the Salvation Army or some other secondhand store, and that stuff on the Busterson family was in there and had to be torn out."

Viola rejected the secondhand Bible possibility out of hand. Because she was older than Lettie and had spent more time in the Deep South than she had, Viola knew that black folks down there, even the very poor ones, would never use a secondhand Bible as their family Bible. They might use a hand-me-down Bible as a going-to-church Bible or as an extra Bible to have around the house, but never as the family Bible. The family Bible was simply too important not to be new.

Seeing that her big sister didn't buy that explanation, Lettie said, "I'll call some of the folks I met at the family reunion and see what I can find out."

"Perhaps you better," Vi said, rolling her eyes.

Lettie's face brightened again. "You remember Uncle Claude, don't you Vi? He was at the family reunion." She had almost forgotten something that she had been dying to tell her sister.

"You mean Uncle Claude from Detroit? I thought he was dead," Vi said.

"Other than having to use a cane and blindness in one eye, he looks good for his age. He had news about Aunt Cecilia."

Lettie was too young to have really known Aunt Cecilia, but Viola knew her. Aunt Cecilia was their mother's favorite aunt who had dropped off the family's radar screen many years ago. Most in the family believed she was dead. For Lettie, Aunt Cecilia was only an unremembered person among many unremembered people in their oral family history.

For Viola, however, Aunt Cecilia was a real flesh-and-blood person from her past. A beloved person. Though she only vaguely remembered Aunt Cecilia, Viola could recall the wisps of expensive perfume that always wafted into the room whenever that white woman, who everyone said was her aunt from Ohio, would walk into the room on one of her rare visits to town. Aunt Cecilia had always been sort of a mystery woman. Even the way she dressed was strange and otherworldly. Then there was that exquisite perfume of hers. Viola remembered as a small girl that friendly smile and those white red-tipped hands that used to gently lift her up onto her silky lap where she, little Viola, loved fondling that beautiful emerald brooch that dangled from Aunt Cecilia's slender white neck. She remembered those kind smiling eyes that were like luminous pools of gray mist.

She also remembered the wonderful gifts that the white woman, who everyone said was her aunt, brought them every time she visited. Such as that fancy cowboy suit, complete with cowboy boots, holsters and pearl-handled toy revolvers, that she once brought their cousin Roger James, who was Aunt Cecilia's favorite of all her nieces and nephews. The year of the cowboy suit was the year when young Viola learned that the tall attractive white woman wasn't white at all, but a black woman who only looked Caucasian.

Most of all, Viola remembered how Aunt Cecilia would disappear as quickly and mysteriously as she had appeared, and how the years would roll by before anyone in the family would see or hear from her again.

"I wonder why Uncle Claude was the only person that Aunt Cecilia kept in contact with all these years," Viola asked.

"Aunt Cecilia didn't stay in contact with Uncle Claude," Lettie said from information obtained at the family reunion, "When she died she left Roger James some money in her will, and it took her estate years to track Roger James down. You know how often he moved around after he got out of the army and after all those divorces of his. Well anyway, one of the attorney's letters finally reached Uncle Claude who sent it to Roger James, who was living in a cheap rooming house in Detroit at the time. Poor Roger James. He was nearly homeless when he learned that Aunt Cecilia had left him all that money."

"How much did she leave him?" Viola asked. She thought of Aunt Cecilia's beautiful emerald brooch she admired so much when she was a little girl. For a split second she felt little-girl pangs of jealousy that the brooch hadn't been left to her. She wasn't surprised, though, that Aunt Cecilia had remembered Roger James in her will. Aunt Cecilia adored cute little Roger James. He was always her favorite, and all the other children in the family knew it.

"$250,000," Lettie said with a giant grin.

"$250,000 to Roger James?" Viola exclaimed with big eyes, "Didn't Aunt Cecilia leave any family of her own?"

"She died with a large family in Cleveland, including some

grandchildren and great grandchildren. Nevertheless, she didn't forget Roger James. She died a widow. Her husband was a wealthy white doctor in Cleveland who left her quite well off. Both of her children are successful physicians."

Lettie laughed, "Girl, Aunt Cecilia had been passing for white for decades. Her Cleveland family is white. She was a respected member of Cleveland's high society. For years she served on many boards of Cleveland's major cultural institutions, including the symphony orchestra. No one knew or suspected she was black."

This news about Aunt Cecilia's "passing" didn't surprise Viola. Being younger, Lettie wasn't as familiar with the concept of "passing" as Viola was. Even when Viola was a small child, many in the family suspected that Aunt Cecilia was passing for white somewhere. "I'm her sister and she doesn't even stay in contact with me," Aunt Chloe said about Cecilia. "I think that child's passing for white somewhere up North, and she doesn't want it known that her family's black. That's why she quietly sneaks in and out of town bearing gifts whenever her conscience gets the best of her."

Viola had heard Aunt Belle say similar things about the many light-skinned blacks that she, Aunt Belle, knew who had changed their race and moved quietly into the white world for a more privileged life as a white person. "Shucks, that's nothing new. Every year since slavery Negroes have passed by the thousands into the white race. After more than three hundred years, if you ran the numbers, it would be hard to find a white person in the United States who didn't have some black blood in them," Aunt Belle said once.

Lettie continued the story, "Uncle Claude said that when Roger James went to Cleveland to sign the papers to get his money, he met Aunt Cecilia's white family at the lawyer's office. They nearly fainted when this big black man walked in and said he was Cecilia Chambers' nephew mentioned in her will."

Lettie turned vinegary and said, "Roger James said that not only were Aunt Cecilia's children white, but by their hostile reaction to him, they seemed like racial bigots. He said at first he thought they were going to refuse to give him his money. Then the lawyer took the white family into another office and talked to them for a long time in private. When they came out of their meeting, the women were crying, and the men glared at him like they wanted to kill him. Roger James thinks the reason they paid him his money without a court fight was that they wanted him out of town as quickly as possible before he embarrassed their family. Girl, white people are a bitch!"

Lettie got up to leave.

"You better get busy on this right away," Viola said, getting back to their family Bible, referring to the telephone calls Lettie said she would make.

"I'll do it after supper," Lettie promised her sister as she was going out the door.

That night before going to bed, Viola Flowers wondered to whom Aunt Cecilia had left that exquisite emerald brooch. The little girl inside of her thought it should have been left to her. It made her feel rather sad.

****

Rev. Viola Flowers had trouble going to sleep that night. Those missing pages upset her very much. She didn't know why. It was just a feeling. For some reason it brought to mind things Aunt Belle said when she was alive. On those trips back to Georgia as a child, little Viola and Aunt Belle talked a lot about many different things, particularly when out hunting mustard greens and wild berries.

Even back then she suspected that Aunt Belle had something on her mind that she wanted to share with her. Sometimes when just the two of them were walking along the railroad tracks talking, Aunt Belle would start to say something, then stop in mid sentence, and her eyes would glaze over and take on a frightened look of someone remembering something very unpleasant. She would give little Viola a funny look like she was wrestling with whether or not to share a dark secret with a mere child. Then her old black face would become smooth and pleasant again. She would pat little Viola on her head and say, "Someday when you're older, I'll tell you about it." She would change the subject as they would trudge along the railroad tracks looking for berries for a pie for supper.

Viola always assumed that what Aunt Belle wanted to tell her had something to do with the family. But they never had that talk. Aunt Belle died, perhaps taking the secret with her. Maybe that Bible held the answer. Maybe that was why Aunt Belle kept it wrapped carefully in silk all those years. Maybe the Bustersons were involved.

When she told her sister about that bit of information earlier, Lettie didn't take it seriously. "So what if there's some big dark secret in our family? Most families have secrets," was Lettie's unconcerned reply.

Thankful Lettie was going to look into it," Viola sighed before rolling over so she could go to sleep.

Chapter Three

Rev. Viola Flowers was called to the ministry at a very early age, preaching her first sermon at age nine. Both her father and grandfather were prominent preachers. Her deceased grandfather, the Bishop T. J. Crombie, was legendary in the gospel world. Her father, the Rev. Tom Crombie, was quite well regarded in his own right. Before Lettie was born, young Viola traveled a lot with her father.

Because she was older, Viola had spent more time in Georgia with their Aunt Belle than Lettie had, and she knew the old ways of the South better than her younger sister did, which was why she doubted that their family Bible had been a secondhand Bible. "In the old days, if black folks owned nothing else new, they would make whatever financial sacrifices necessary to own a new Bible to use as the family Bible," Aunt Belle told her once, pointing out that other than birth and death certificates, the family Bible was the most official document that most black households possessed.

She told young Viola how white salesmen used to travel around the South selling new Bibles door-to-door to black folks on credit, requiring so much down and so much every month until the Bible was paid for. The salesmen would come around every month and collect their money, from as little as a quarter to a few dollars a month, depending on the family's income. "Black folks never defaulted on their Bible bills. They were too afraid of what God would think," Aunt Belle laughed.

To illustrate her point about the importance of the family Bible in those days, Aunt Belle told young Viola this story: "Back then black families often used the family Bible in court to prove such things as heirship and paternity. There was this little girl whose unwed mother was killed in a car accident. The state wanted to put the little girl in an orphanage. The girl's father was a married man. Nearly everyone in the black community knew who the girl's father was, including the married man's wife. When the child was born, the couple nearly divorced because of it.

"Nonetheless, when the married man's wife heard about the

fatal accident and that the little girl had been placed in an orphanage, she made her husband step up and take responsibility for his own flesh and blood. 'It's me and the children who must suffer all the shame for what you did, not you. Everybody in town knows you have trouble keeping your hands off young women. But the fact remains. The child's yours. And we can't stand by and allow that poor child to become an orphan. She belongs here with her brothers and sisters,' the wife severely chastised her husband.

"She made him go downtown and claim his child. She went with him. But because the little girl's paternity hadn't been proven in a court, they were required to petition the family court, where their family Bible was successfully used to prove the paternity. Fortunately when the wife first learned of her husband's love child and he admitted it, she listed the child in their family Bible along with their children. 'It's the only Christian thing to do,' she told him when she forgave him for his infidelity that day."

Aunt Mildred was the only relative on their father's side who stayed in Georgia. When young she lived up North for awhile, but moved back to Georgia where she spent the rest of her life. Viola loved visiting her in Georgia, and enjoyed working in the fields with her.

Because Aunt Belle attended high school for awhile in the North where she took a Red Cross first-aid course, she was the closest thing in that part of rural Georgia that black folks had as a doctor or nurse. Since the nearest hospital was nearly fifty miles away, and because the one white doctor in the area wouldn't take black patients, black folks in the area called on her for their health care needs that ranged from earaches to ptomaine poisoning. With her herbs, home remedies, medical books, and the little bit of real medicine that she remembered from her Red Cross training, Aunt Belle tried to help them the best she could, and eventually she even made a decent living at it. Even some poor whites came to her with their ailments. Over time she got her license and retired as a highly regarded county nurse.

Besides being a nurse, Aunt Belle was a truck farmer who grew so much fruit and vegetables on her small plot of land that what she didn't eat or canned for herself she sent to the market in town. She told young Viola about how in the old days an old farmer would stop by on Tuesdays with his horse and wagon, put her bushel baskets of fruits and vegetable on his wagon alongside his own produce, and take them into town and sell them for her. What he sold of hers, they split the profits, which helped augment Aunt Belle's modest income.

At the time Lettie was too young to make trips South to visit Aunt Belle.

Chapter Four

Rev. Flowers was very tired when she returned home from making her hospital rounds. It had been emotionally wrenching watching Sister Grimes lay there in the hospital like that, all tubed up and wasted away to just skin and bones. Sister Grimes was the same woman who only six short months ago was vibrant and robust and headed the church's Sunday school program. Then she suddenly fell ill from cancer and was now on the brink of death. Today at the hospital Rev. Flowers prayed for her until she herself became very exhausted, and for the sake of her own health she had to leave and go home.

The first thing Viola did when back in her study was to drop to her knees and pray. She asked God for renewed strength so she could continue to do the work of her ministry, which seemed to be getting harder every day. "O Lord, life's so hard for so many of my parishioners. Sometimes I feel so helpless in the face of all the hardships and problems that so many of them must face every day. Please give me the strength to help them with their problems," she prayed.

She was referring to how many of her parishioners were being struck down in the prime of life due to poor or neglected health. From the pulpit she could detect the members who weren't taking care of themselves. She could see the obesity because of poor eating, particularly the children. She could see the neglected teeth and the red-veined eyes that suggested untreated high-blood pressure. She could hear the panting and heavy breathing that hinted asthma or just the lack of exercise. What was extra worrisome was that many of her parishioners didn't have health insurance. She personally knew that many of her old people had failing health because they couldn't afford their medicine. While on her knees she would always ask God why a society as rich as ours wasn't doing more in that regard.

She heard the front door open and thought it was her sister Lettie who was expected to drop by that afternoon. "Hi, Ma. I can't stay long," Maxine said as she came through the door. It was Viola and Albert Flowers' grown daughter, their only child. "I got the promotion!" she told her mother excitedly.

"That's great, honey. That calls for a celebration," Viola said with a big smile.

Rev. Flowers was very proud of Maxine. For a long time after graduating from high school, Maxine seemed unable to get her life unstuck. She seemed not to know what to do with her life. Despite getting good grades in high school she never had any interest in going to college as her parents had wanted. She was unable to keep a steady job, and kept coming back home to live whenever she encountered financial difficulties. The last time was the third time she had U-hauled back home and reclaimed her old room. It wasn't that Maxine was lazy. On the contrary. She always worked. It was only that she kept hopping from one low entry-level job to another. Her life was like a pilotless motor boat going around and around on a small lake. For awhile Rev. Flowers feared she might be on drugs.

"I don't know what we're going to do with that girl. She's so irresponsible. Mr. Burrell called me this afternoon and told me that she didn't show up for her interview," Rev. Flowers decried to Albert one day back when they were having trouble with Maxine. Viola was furious because Maxine had failed to keep a job interview at her bank that she had set up with the branch manager. Back then Maxine seemed unable to keep appointments.

"Don't worry about Maxine, Vi. Like so many young people these days, she's trying to find herself," Albert tried to reassure his worried wife about their daughter.

Then almost miraculously Maxine got her life together when one day she fell madly in love with a job that she was sent to by her temp agency. This assignment resulted in a permanent position eighteen months later, followed by promotion after promotion in the company. "I told you that she was just trying to find herself," Albert said to Viola proudly about the way their daughter had straightened her life out.

Viola and Maxine sat in the kitchen and talked.

"I gotta go. I didn't realize it was so late," Maxine said after looking at the clock.

"What's your hurry? Your Aunt Lettie is stopping by in a little while. Maybe she'll take us out to celebrate your promotion." She was alluding to Lettie's legendary generosity.

"I can't. Some friends and I are going to a concert tonight at the Hollywood Bowl. Before going home to change, I must stop by the liquor store. My friends are bringing the dinner baskets and I'm bringing the wine," Maxine told her mother. "By the way, may I borrow your black leather jacket. The Bowl gets a little chilly when the sun goes down." She was speaking of the outdoors concerts at the Hollywood Bowl.

"It's in my upstairs clothes closet. Help yourself."

When Maxine came back downstairs with the jacket, she said, "I don't know why you don't wear this jacket more. You look so foxy in it."

"It was a gift, but it's too daring for me to wear. I'm a minister of the gospel, not a Hollywood starlet."

"Ma, you're a beautiful, voluptuous woman. You should stop trying to hide that fact," Maxine said as she rushed for the door.

****

Moments after Maxine left, Rev. Flowers' sister Lettie dropped by. Viola was at the kitchen sink washing the cups that she and Maxine had used. She stopped what she was doing and dried her hands.

"Well, what did you find out?" she asked Lettie anxiously, more certain than ever that the so-called family Bible represented some kind of danger to them.

Lettie had called Viola earlier in the day and said she would drop by after work to report on what she had learned thus far about the Busterson family, reporting that she had made the telephone calls as promised, but none of the relatives she contacted knew anything about the Bustersons, which meant she had to dig deeper. Because she planned to do a family tree of the family in any event, she decided to embark upon it immediately. The research might shed some light on who the Bustersons were, she figured.

"I could find nothing on the Bustersons in Georgia on Daddy's side of the family. I did everything Gladys told me to do. I worked backwards as she said I should do, first getting information from older relatives who are still alive. That's why I've been making all those long-distance telephone calls," Lettie said.

"Who's Gladys?" Vi asked.

"She's the friend of mine who traced her Scottish ancestors back nine generations to a relative in Scotland she believes was the Bishop of Aberdeen in 1207. She began by reading a book on how to research her European ancestry, and then started her research by visiting her great grandfather's Civil War grave in the Shenandoah Valley, and getting information from his tombstone."

"I'm sure there're no books on how to research our African ancestry," Rev. Flowers said facetiously.

"That's not true, Vi. You'd be surprised. Since Alex Haley's novel *Roots*, there's much material now on how to trace African American families. There's a book by a guy in Detroit who traced his family back ten generations to Africa. The probate records in Mississippi led him to the shipping records, and the shipping records led him to West Africa."

"West Africa?" Vi's eyes got large.

"Yes. His research led him there. He ended up going to Nigeria and speaking to griots up and down the coast looking for his roots. They sent him inland where he finally found his relatives in an Ibo village."

Lettie explained, "The census records in the county where his family lived listed all the members of his great grandfather's household by name, age, and county of birth. He followed the census records back as far as he could, which took him back to the days of slavery. Then he turned to the probate records of the white people who owned his relatives when they were slaves. Remember, Vi, slaves were considered personal property, and on their owner's death, they passed through probate just like any other piece of property. Like horses and cows. In their wills white families usually described their slaves in great detail so there wouldn't be any mix-up about which slave or group of slaves went where upon the slave master's death."

Lettie glanced nervously at the clock. "The African American genealogical guides warn that when you get back to slavery times in your research it's important that you start tracing the family back through the mothers. Often black fathers were unacknowledged, especially to the white folks in the big house who did all the recordkeeping. Remember, everything a slave did had to have the consent of the white master, even romance and sex."

Lettie then added, "What's more, often the father of the black woman's child was the white slave owner himself. White men were notorious in those days for taking sexual liberties with their female slaves. Making slaves from their own semen was an inexpensive way for them to increase their slave holdings without spending a dime. This was a big problem for white families in those days. It probably wasn't easy for the white children knowing that all those little yellow Negroes running around the plantation were their half brothers and sisters."

Viola could see Lettie had done much reading on the subject.

Lettie let go a big erumpent laugh, "Shit. Haven't you heard of animal husbandry? No wonder most of us African Americans are so racially mixed."

Rev. Flower gave Lettie that reproving look she gave people who used profanity in her presence, yet she couldn't stop the corners of her mouth from curling up.

Viola spoke up impatiently, "We aren't looking for our roots. We're just looking to see what the Bustersons had to do with our family."

"I realize that, Vi, but the principles involved are the same."

"Did you use one of those genealogy books in your research? Did you check both names?" Vi asked, thinking Lettie's job should be much easier than the job the man in Detroit had, inasmuch as Lettie didn't have to go all the way back to Africa in her research. She only had to go a few decades into Georgia.

"Yes, but I couldn't find anything in our genealogy on the Bustersons," Lettie answered, "The State Historical Society helped me find quite a bit on Daddy, however. They have a large collection of newspapers on microfilm. They sent me a copy of Daddy's obituary, but it contained nothing we didn't already know. The same was true of grandpa's obituary that they faxed me from Missouri. It didn't contain much either. The librarian says that to do a real thorough search we should check the public records in Georgia."

Viola got to her feet. "I'm going to St. Louis for the Midwest Conference in a couple of weeks. When the conference is over, I'll fly to Georgia and see what I can find. I've a couple of days I can spare. Give me a list of what I should look for."

Rev. Flowers felt it was important that she go to Georgia as soon as possible, because everyday their chances lessened of finding someone still alive who could shed some light on their family history on their father's side. Someone who might know why those pages were ripped from the family Bible.

She would first visit Aunt Jennie to see what she knew. Aunt Jennie lived near Aunt Belle in the South, and over the years she visited her whenever she could. The two women were quite close. In fact, Aunt Jennie thought of Aunt Belle as her own aunt. In Aunt Belle's ailing years, because no other family member was around, Aunt Jennie was the one who put the old lady in a nursing home when the latter could no longer care for herself. Aunt Belle was nearly a hundred years old when she died.

After seeing Aunt Jennie, she would search the public records of the county where their grandfather was born to see what she could find out there.

"I'll prepare a list for you before you leave. I gotta run." Lettie got up from the kitchen table. Before leaving she turned and said, "That was a terrific show you did last week."

****

Lettie was referring to her sister's radio show. Rev. Flowers was proud of the gospel radio show she hosted every Sunday that was one of the longest running religious programs of its kind in Southern California. The pay was meager but she found hosting the show to be fun. It also helped her to grow her church. Her radio show stemmed from the Watts Riots in the 1960s during the high point of the Civil Rights Movement in the United States when African Americans took to the streets to protest for their equal rights. During that period race riots rocked America, and Los Angeles was no exception. For six days blacks torched and looted the Negro community of Los Angeles called Watts.

On the first day of the L.A. riots, the white radio station manager at KWCP invited black leaders, particularly leading ministers, to come into the station and go on the air to help quell the racial disturbance. One of the clergy people who responded was Sister Eva Carrie from Temple Baptist Church. While Watts burned Sister Carrie spun gospel records in her radio booth at KWCP, and prayed on the air round the clock for the black people of Watts to come to their senses and stop the rioting. She begged the young men roaming the streets to return to their homes and help build their community, instead of destroying it. Many of those young men heeded her plea and got off the streets.

Sister Carrie became so popular in South-Central Los Angeles that the radio station gave her a weekly gospel show that ran for years until she suddenly dropped dead one day from a heart attack. Then Rev. Flowers took over the weekly radio show and its success continued to grow. Under her, the show became famous for its great gospel music, its religious public service announcements, and its sincere over-the-air prayers for the sick, the shut-ins, and the homeless. Rev. Flowers even prayed for men and women in prison; in fact she prayed on the air for anyone who requested it.

The two greatest fans of Rev. Flowers' radio show were Walter and Fumiko Matsui, Viola Flowers' next door neighbors. The Matsui family loved the gospel music played at Rev. Flowers' church. Fumiko's Japanese American parents had lived in that neighborhood long before World War II, and were among the thousands of Japanese Americans rounded up during America's war with Japan and Germany, and shipped to relocation camps where her parents were held for nearly three years. Sadly Fumiko Matsui died last year.

One day last year when going to her car parked in her driveway, Rev. Flowers saw Fumiko as she was returning from her daily walk. She knew Fumiko was receiving treatments for cancer. Despite the 80-degree weather that day, Fumiko was wearing large dark sunglasses, a wide felt hat, a heavy pea coat, leather gloves, and was all bundled up in a wool scarf like it was sub-zero weather outside. It was the medication she was taking that had made her so chilly that day. Other than all the clothing, the small sixtyish woman looked very hardy. In truth her cheeks were rosy.

"You look good, Fumiko," Viola Flowers remarked after the two of them stopped and exchanged pleasantries.

"It's my children, Rev. Flowers. They're making me eat. They're making me fat, even though I tell them that I want to die," the little woman said, tearing up. "They don't realize what a struggle it is for me day after day. I have the strength to live, but not the will." She mustered a little Japanese smile. "I think the only reason I open my eyes every morning is that I know Walter will have breakfast waiting for me. He's so sweet the way he looks after me."

The corners of her pale lips fell and the little smile vanished and her face became a chalky white. The "Walter" she meant was Walter Matsui, her husband and retired chemist, who raised rare Japanese plants in their large backyard. Neighbors would sometimes see Mr. Matsui early in the morning backing out of his driveway with his car loaded with plants. They knew he sold his plants somewhere, but no one really knew where. Most of the neighbors conjectured that it was the large flower mart downtown.

Albert, however, was of the opinion that Walter Matsui was selling his plants by catalog, maybe on the internet. "I bet Walt has a website for his catalog business. What a great idea. I wonder if he needs a partner," he commented once, that adventurous entrepreneurial mind of his on full gallop.

"Albert, you leave Mr. Matsui alone," Viola would fuss at him at the time, "He doesn't need you in his business."

Fumiko and Walter Matsui were a very handsome couple. They resembled aging Japanese movies stars. Before Fumiko fell ill, she and Walter loved ballroom dancing and went out dancing nearly every Saturday night. Both were excellent dancers. "Sometimes we dance until dawn," Fumiko told Rev. Flowers once over their back fence.

Now here this beautiful little woman was, standing there talking about having no will to live.

"Would you mind if I said a prayer for you?" Rev. Flowers asked, unsure whether a Christian prayer would be proper since Fumiko Matsui might be Buddhist.

"I haven't been to church in ages, so I guess I could use a little praying for," Fumiko joked feebly.

There on the sidewalk Rev. Flowers took Fumiko's hand and said a little prayer for her. The two of them hugged. Fumiko was so thin and her bones so light that Rev. Flowers had to take care not to bruise her as they stood there embraced.

Then the little Japanese woman planted a tiny cold kiss on Rev. Flowers' cheek and went into her house where her husband Walter had her midmorning soup waiting for her.

Four days later Fumiko Matsui died.

Chapter Five

You had to know Albert Flowers to understand his remark about Walter Matsui's business of raising rare plants. Some years ago after Viola broke up with her longtime boyfriend Rev. Emanuel Scott, a good friend introduced her to her now husband Albert Flowers. "Albert's a good catch, Vi. He has a good-paying job with the county, and he's a high official with the employee's union. Most of all, he's a good church-going man," the friend told her, who had exaggerated a bit since Albert was only the assistant treasurer of his union at the time.

Rev. Flowers met Albert Flowers and liked him. When he asked her to marry him, she had been seeing him for less than six months. It was "seeing" rather than "dating" because that's really what their relationship was in the beginning. They were more like good friends who occasionally went out and did fun things together, nothing physical, albeit she had to slap Albert's hands away a few times. They married in a big church wedding.

Albert Flowers was a chunkily built man with large hands, a round pleasant face, and a big bright politician's smile. Most important, he had a good heart. It didn't matter to her that he wasn't exactly good-looking, because since Manny Scott she didn't trust good-looking men anymore. After Manny Scott she saw handsome men as dangerous Venus Fly Traps whose beautiful pedals were only there to attract prey. Everything about her relationship with Manny Scott had been extra intense—their times alone, their times out together, their deep intellectual discussions, especially on theology, their arguments, their awful fights, and their passionate lovemaking. Therefore, when she and Rev. Scott broke up, meeting a nice, easy-going teddy bear like Albert Flowers was a welcome change. Fun-loving, Albert always made her laugh, whereas Manny always made her cry. What impressed her most about Albert was his large ambition. She saw him as a man who wanted to do something with his life. He wasn't full of crap like Manny.

One day a couple of years ago Rev. Flowers and Albert

attended a citywide evangelical conference of mostly white fundamentalist churches. At the conference Albert met and became bosom buddies with some white born-again men. His new white Christian friends even asked him to join the white Kiwanis Club, where he took up cigar smoking. It was at the Kiwanis Club where he met and became good friends with Bob Haines, a lifelong Republican from Culver City, who later became his business partner. The Kiwanis Club led to Albert's joining other white civic and social organizations.

"I didn't know white people could be so friendly," he told Viola about his new conservative friends when he returned home one day with a bag of golf clubs that one of them had given him. When Vi asked him if he had taken up golfing now, he replied, "Ralph's teaching me. We're teeing off tomorrow morning at the country club at seven," he said with a big smile.

Eventually Albert saw less and less of his old black friends as he spent more time with his new born-again white buddies. It wasn't long before he went into business with one of them. When that business failed, he and another white friend, Bob Haines, established a shuttle service that they managed to get into LAX through certain political connections Bob Haines had at City Hall.

Albert considered the day he first met Bob Haines and his other new white Christian friends the luckiest day of his life. It was at a social during an evangelical conference that he and Viola had attended in Hawthorne, a small city a few miles south of Los Angeles. The people there were mostly white born-again Christians. At the social, the men of the group, including Albert Flowers, gathered outside for smokes, where they talked a lot about entrepreneurship. Most of them owned or aspired to own their own businesses. Albert was amazed when one of the white men turned to him in a friendly way and asked matter-of-factly, "What line of business are you in, Al?"

Albert was in hog heaven. He had found his tribe. Here was a group of men who thought like he did on most issues, and among those guys, having one's own business was the natural order of things. Because he was there, everyone just assumed he was a businessman also.

Another thing, with his new conservative friends, unlike when around his white liberal and progressive friends, his race seemed immaterial. All that mattered to them was that he too loved making money, and that seemed to be enough. What a rare wonderful experience for a black man! Albert Flowers was so happy that he was nearly moved to tears. He had found his real home. A place where he didn't have to be ashamed of his love for business. He was now among men who appreciated the excitement of putting together a business plan and watching the business move towards success. They were men with whom he could share his dreams. Men who knew what a bottom line was.

Albert saw them as men who were brave, strong and determined, all qualities he admired in people. A few of them had gone through bankruptcy, not once but several times, and, still unfazed, were starting over in business again.

"While sitting there in bankruptcy court waiting for my case to be called, I thought of this great new idea on how to get back into business again. I couldn't wait to be declared bankrupt so I could get back into action again. This time, though, I decided to keep my in-laws out of it. It was my goddamn brother-in-law who ruined my last business. I shouldn't have listened to my wife when she begged me to put him in charge of sales. That four-flusher even gave me a phony resume. Can you imagine that, my own brother-in-law. When that lazy bastard should've been out on the road taking care of business, he'd be holed up in a bar somewhere getting smash. I should've fired the sonofabitch the first week I hired him," one of Albert's new friends said about a new business he was planning, who even had his new investment capital all lined up.

Those men were why Albert became a Republican. He now often reflected back with regret why he remained a Democrat for as long as he did. He was definitely convinced that white Republicans, unlike white liberals and progressives, didn't mind if a black man made a little money for himself, and they would accept you if you showed some get-up-and-go about yourself. He later went into business with a couple of those white men, but their business failed, and he learned a lot from that experience. Then Albert tried again with another white partner, this time with Bob Haines and their airport shuttle van business.

Albert Flowers was one of capitalism's most ardent spokesmen. He constantly championed owning one's own business. "The Free

Enterprise System gives everyone with a little personal savings the chance to take a sound idea and open his or her own business, with the sky being the limit," he would tell people who would listen to him. For folks serious about starting their own business, he would dive enthusiastically into their plans like they were his own. A small businessman himself, Albert was always the first to applaud someone for trying to get ahead in life.

Take Alfredo Cortez, for example. Alfredo Cortez was the Flowers' Mexican American neighbor, who lived a few doors down from them with his young wife and two small children. Albert Flowers admired the young man for working so hard in trying to establish his own businesses. By day Alfredo worked for a well-known landscaping service, but evenings he ran his own little grass-cutting business, sometimes working until it was almost too dark to see. One of his duties on his regular job was to take his employer's truck at the break of dawn every day and pick up other employees who didn't have transportation and bring them to the employer's place of business, where they would assemble in teams to go out for the day. Ergo Alfredo was allowed to take the company truck home at nights.

One day he told Vi and Albert Flowers why he worked so hard. It was all a part of his plan to get ahead in life, he told them, which delighted Albert. Having his employer's truck to use overnight enabled Alfredo to run his own little gardening business after he got off work evenings. At first he had planned to work at his regular job only until he could afford to buy his own pickup truck. Then his young wife became pregnant with their first child which made saving for his truck even more difficult. Then came the second child, closely followed by the need to buy a house. However, instead of abandoning his dream of being self-employed, Alfredo just worked longer and harder.

Therefore, every day after a full day of back-breaking lawn work on his regular job, he would rush home, have a quick meal, load his lawn mowers into his pickup truck, pick up his brother and some teenage cousins, and then go out and service his own customers in the little daylight left.

"Vi, when does that kid find time to sleep?" Albert would say, amazed when he would come home late at night and see Alfredo Cortez working with a flashlight under the hood of the truck.

"Where does Alfredo get the energy to work all those long hard hours?" Viola Flowers would reply as she worried about his health. In many ways the young man reminded her of Albert.

Happily the day came when Alfredo got his new truck, purchased a nice house across the street from his parents, and quit his regular job and devoted himself exclusively to his own flourishing business. Albert was as proud of him as he would have been of his own son.

Or take Maria Sanchez, another example, who was a coworker of Albert's at the county building. Knowing how strongly Al Flowers felt about people starting their own businesses, Maria talked to him one day in confidence about her salsa sauce. "Everybody who's tasted my sauce tells me how good it is, and that I should sell it in the supermarkets," she told him at work that day.

Albert was her union shop steward at the time. He thought her idea was a good one and encouraged her to give it a try; he even helped her with her business plan. She took his advice, got her business going, and it did great. Eventually, to get more space she moved the business out of her small East Los Angeles home and into her garage, and hired her uncle to run the plant as foreman.

Then thanks to the Internet, her sales grew so fast that she soon became faced with the inevitable decision of when to quit her relatively secure civil service job to run her business full time. With Albert's encouragement, she took the fateful plunge and quit her job. Albert was pleased by her success almost as much as she was.

Ambitious folks like Alfredo Cortez and Maria Sanchez were Al Flowers' kind of people.

Chapter Six

Albert Flowers was the world's greatest salesman for entrepreneurialism. In fact it was his passionate entrepreneurial spirit that finally drew him, a Democrat, to the Republicans. Despite that his old Democratic friends shared his liberal concerns for the disadvantaged and the poor, most of them lacked his enthusiasm for capitalism, which he saw as a great system.

"If you're going into business when you retire, you need to start planning now," he would tell his coworkers before reciting a litany of things that must be considered, the most important being having adequate capital. "Start saving now," he would advise them.

While Albert loved helping people with their business ideas, he didn't suffer idle dreamers and windbags well, and if he felt a coworker was just shooting the bull with him about going into business, he would move away briskly, because he had better ways to spend his time. Albert saw no ideological conflict in his love of business with his support for strong unions. Indeed he believed that strong, honest unions made companies stronger, not weaker. He believed they improved morale, which in turn increased productivity, and that increased productivity, he believed, should be shared by Labor and Capital fairly. Even today on this point he still had heated arguments with his Republican buddies, most of whom hated unions and believed in "trickle-down "economics. He also saw no conflict between owning a business and having humanitarian concerns for the working class.

"It absolutely makes no sense in a country as wealthy as ours to have all the poverty and hunger that we have. In fact, it's a drag on the economy," he would say when agreeing with his Democratic friends in the old days. Then he would quickly add, "I agree with you that government has a role to play in helping the black community, but our community also needs capital so black folks can start their own businesses and redevelop their own neighborhoods. It's true that banks have discriminated against us black folks for years, holding us back, but things have gotten much better now. More of us, especially our young people, should take advantage of these new opportunities and go into business for ourselves." Albert Flowers was the world's greatest optimist.

His old Democratic buddies weren't necessarily hostile to the idea of a black man owning his own business per se. It was only that, to them, this seemed such a feeble way to help the vast majority of black folks with their massive social problems. One friend, questioning the Free Enterprise System's ability to solve social problems, argued, "The Free Market, Al, is driven only by profits, and if something isn't profitable, than the Market wants no part of it. There're no profits in helping the poor, not even for politicians, so everybody runs from that issue."

Furthermore, because most black businesses were barely surviving, many of Albert's old Democratic friends thought it was the height of folly for anyone to quit a good-paying job to open some shaky little business that would probably never get off the ground. Some had unkind things to say about the black businesses that were very successful, "The first thing a successful black businessman does when he makes a little money is to move out of the black community to a wealthier section of the city, usually a white section, leaving his old neighborhood even weaker. Often they change their political affiliation," an old friend of his said once.

When Albert worked for the county government, most of his friends thought he was crazy to leave such a cushy, civil service job to enter the risky, dangerous world of private business. They thought he was crazy for risking his life savings. They all knew how difficult savings were to come by in the black community. "What's your hurry, Al? Why don't you wait until you retire so you'll at least have your full pension to fall back on if things don't turn out as planned," many of his friends and coworkers told him, wanting to keep him from harming himself.

Even his wife secretly felt that way. From the start, while wanting to be supportive, Viola had her qualms about Albert's leaving his good Los Angeles County job for a risky business venture like that. She didn't see why that was necessary at that point in the business. She knew many people, including members of her church, who held their jobs while running small businesses on the side. Take Brother Holmes, for example. During the day he worked full time at the Hughes Aircraft plant, and at night he ran his small machine shop on Venice Boulevard that was growing so fast that he now had four employees.

"I could really leaves Hughes right now, Rev. Flowers, but having a paycheck coming in regularly from my job has helped bail my little business out so many times that I hate giving that job up. But I guess soon I'll have to. My business has reached a point where staying at Hughes is now costing me money," he told her a few months before he quit his job in favor of full time at his machine shop. He said he prayed over it and God told him it was the wise thing to do. Elder Holmes was just one of the many people Viola knew who had jobs while trying to establish their own businesses.

There were many times when Viola wished Albert would have kept his government job a little longer. He had owned other businesses while keeping his job, but those businesses were minor and only part-time. With the shuttle business he was forced to retire early from his job because as a condition of their SBA loan, one of the partners had to manage the business on a full-time basis. Since Bob Haines had his hands full with other things at the time, the responsibility fell on Albert. Because the bank loaned them less operating capital than they requested, Albert's paychecks from the shuttle business were spotty at best in the first couple of years in business. God how they missed those steady government paychecks then. Albert's retirement checks didn't come close to filling the gap. During that period most of the family's income came from Viola's meager salary as pastor of their church.

This attitude of Albert's friends and coworkers was very discouraging for him. Even worse, it was very intimidating. For aspiring entrepreneurs, fear held by friends and loved ones can be as contagious as measles. Consequently, due to the timidity around him that even frightened him a little, Albert stayed on his job many years longer than he had planned. At that time had he been around bold, business-minded people like Bob Haines and his friends, he likely would have left his job much earlier, he believed.

Chapter Seven

Bernice Jones was Rev. Flowers' longtime hairdresser and good friend. The two of them met some years ago when Viola Flowers first moved to Los Angeles to establish her church. Being new to the city and needing a good hairdresser, Rev. Flowers asked around and someone told her about this black hairdresser named Bernice, who was said to be not only very good but very cheap. That Bernice was cheap was a big selling point with Viola Flowers because she was just starting out on her own and had to watch her spending. Bernice then was doing people's hair in her kitchen. Rev. Flowers had been warned that Bernice Jones was a little flaky and very unreliable.

Rev. Flowers tried her, liked the way she did her hair, and used her ever since, but it wasn't easy. Because she constantly struggled to pay her rent, Bernice moved around a great deal without bothering to tell her customers, so it was hard to keep track of her.

In the early days of their relationship, several times Rev. Flowers literally had to track Bernice down to get her hair done. That Bernice's telephone stayed disconnected for long periods due to unpaid phone bills didn't help matters any. Unable to contact her on the telephone, Viola would go to Bernice's house or shop (if she had a shop) expecting to get her hair done, and find that Bernice was no longer there. Usually the new occupant had no idea where Bernice had moved to.

Bernice was so whimsical in how she ran her business that it never occurred to her that she had an obligation when she moved her shop to notify her customers, particularly her regulars like Rev. Flowers. But because Bernice was so good, and not wanting to get a new hairdresser, most of her customers, including Rev. Flowers, always made the effort to find her. So like a private detective, Rev. Flowers hunted Bernice down and followed her to ten different locations over the years.

Once when Bernice was missing, someone told Rev. Flowers that they thought Bernice had move to somewhere in the Crenshaw area. So one day Rev. Flowers went to that area and walked around and looked for her, checking shops and looking desultorily through plate-glass windows. Then all of a sudden, someone stuck her head out the door of a low-rent storefront across the street and yelled, "Vi!"

Rev. Flowers stopped and looked, and there was Bernice in the doorway, with a big grin on her face and a pair of scissors in her hand. "I wondered what happened to you," she told Rev. Flowers nonchalantly when the latter was snugly ensconced in the chair. Bernice always made it sound like it was Viola Flowers who had disappeared without telling anybody. "That's Bernice," Rev. Flowers would chuckle when discussing Bernice with others.

Their friendship was an odd one, she a gospel minister, and Bernice a nonbeliever who didn't believe in an afterlife, which was rare for an African American woman. "I believe when you're dead, you're dead," the high school dropout told Rev. Flowers earlier in their relationship. Although Rev. Flowers' job was converting nonbelievers into believers, she never tried to convert Bernice. She knew better. Also she liked Bernice exactly as she was. While Viola Flowers would likely deny it, Bernice's irreverence was probably one of the reasons she was so drawn to her. With Bernice there were never any moralistic judgments, just straight talk.

It was true that Rev. Flowers worried a great deal about Bernice's soul and prayed for her a lot. She particularly worried about Bernice's gambling habits. Bernice's favorite pastime was playing the ponies every day and going to Las Vegas when she could. She loved staying and gambling at Caesars Palace. Nonetheless, Viola Flowers liked and trusted Bernice.

There were few secrets between her and Bernice. They talked on the telephone several times a week. More than with anyone else she knew, Rev. Flowers felt perfectly safe telling Bernice personal things about herself that she wouldn't dare tell anyone else, not even her husband Albert or her sister Lettie. Things about herself that were almost too embarrassing for her to admit to.

Once, for instance, Rev. Flowers admitted to Bernice her fears of running into Manny at conferences and other religious gatherings when she was out of town alone. "Manny can bring the devil out in me like no one else can," she told Bernice that day, half joking, half serious. She also confessed to Bernice that she often fantasized about Manny when having sex with Albert.

"Vi, it's only natural that you still feel that way about him," Bernice wisecracked, "He busted your cherry, for heaven's sake. I think about that little boy next door who busted mine all the time. So give him some pussy, gal, so you can get on with your life. Albert's not going to miss any." It was a remark that made Viola and Manny's relationship sound much simpler than it really was.

Another time, she told Bernice about the time in Bible college when she thought she was pregnant with Manny's child, and actually thought of getting an abortion.

"When I learned later that I wasn't pregnant, I dropped to my knees and begged Jesus to forgive me for entertaining such a wicked notion. It took me quite awhile to get over that. For awhile I actually considered going into therapy. That was the worst period of my life," Viola said sadly. She told Bernice that for a long time thereafter she refused to let Manny touch her sexually. She even admitted to Bernice that Manny and Albert were the only men she had had sex with in her life. Then she said embarrassed, "You're the only person I've ever told that to."

Whenever she had those frank girl-to-girl talks with Bernice, when back home and alone in her office, Rev. Flowers couldn't believe she had told Bernice those things, things she had sworn to herself never to reveal to anyone.

Chapter Eight

Rev. Emanuel Scott was the longtime pastor of the New Era Church of God in Christ in Chicago and was known across the country for his powerful preaching. He and Viola Flowers were lovers in college, and even today her heart still raced a little when she saw him. She first met Manny Scott at a small religious college in Cedar Rapids, Iowa, that they both attended just out of high school. They were only seventeen at the time. He was from a small town near Chicago. They were the only African Americans in their class, indeed in the whole school. They both came from a long line of preachers in the black Holiness Movement, a movement that broke off from the black Baptist Church in the 1890s for overemphasizing holiness. After leaving the Baptist Church, the leaders in the black Holiness Movement had doctrinal differences between themselves and broke into two groups and went their separate ways.

Emanuel's great grandfather stayed in the original group called the Church of God in Christ, the church where his grandfather and father were later ordained. Viola's grandfather, then a young rebellious preacher in the Church of God in Christ, went with the other group that named itself the Church of Christ. Then some years later her grandfather and his followers broke with the Church of Christ largely over the issue of speaking in tongues, and started their own church they called the Church of God & Spirit, where he became the bishop of the church. The subdividing of black Christian holiness churches seemed to never stop. When in college Viola Flowers and Manny Scott talked about the possibility that their grandfathers knew each other in the old days, and perhaps worked or fought with each other.

The doctrine of the Church of God & Spirit was very strict back in the old days. In fact, in those days the Church of God & Spirit resembled the Amish in the sense that the church was very standoffish and distrusting of the outside world, which included mainstream churches. This was a problem for Rev. Flowers when she was given her own church, because she believed in fellowshipping with other churches. And her father, who was a little more broad-minded as a minister than her grandfather, agreed with her, but he warned her not to get too far ahead of her congregants, especially in such things as attending interdenominational and interfaith conferences and conventions. To the old-timers of the church, it was like other churches were fatally diseased, and one had to be careful about bringing those germs back to their church.

Over the years Rev. Flowers tried to lead her church into the light of modern times from the darkness of doctrinaire scripture, but her church was like a huge boulder that was hard to move. At times it seemed the best she could do was to keep trying to nudge her congregation in the right direction. Sometimes she was able to make changes, sometimes she wasn't. Yet she had some successes. For example, by pointing out how the Christian Right always opposed anything that helped ordinary working people, she successfully kept her church from following reactionary white leaders like Rev. Jerry Falwell and Pat Robertson as a few black churches did. Her members appreciated the many gains that labor unions had won for them, and touching Social Security was anathema to them, inasmuch as Social Security was the only thing that the whole black community could really rely on from month to month.

But Viola Flowers knew she had to keep trying. Whenever she thought of the younger members of her church, she felt better. For every year more and more younger members were ascending to positions of leadership in the church. Younger, more progressive-thinking people, more in touch with the times, who wanted to break with old beliefs and traditions. Rev. Flowers saw this as very hopeful.

"Be careful, Viola. In every church there's always a clique that's stuck in the past," her father, who was a minister himself, warned her when he was alive. From the time he took over the church when he was alive, he feared the dissident groups in the Church of God & Spirit that wanted to break away from the national church and form their own churches. And he remained mindful of the fights he and his father had over the years to keep the church in one piece.

"Palace revolts are always brewing in secret somewhere in our religious kingdom," he told his daughter Viola, sounding like a king speaking to his princess.

Chapter Nine

Viola Flowers and Manny Scott's relationship on campus started out on a plutonic basis. Because Manny was so arrogant and cocky on campus, particularly with the girls, Viola disliked him at first. Then she reasoned that because they were the only two black students at the college they should at least be friends. "I guess there's nothing wrong in our being just platonic friend, Emanuel," she told him one day. "But only platonic friends. Nothing more," she warned him. So they became good friends, and became very protective of each other, often studying together. It was amazing how fast they became lovers; brother and sister one moment, and passionate lovers the next. It happened just that quickly.

Even today Rev. Flowers felt immense shame just thinking about all the sinning she and Manny did in college in the name of love. In particular she recalled the time when she and Manny Scott made love on the library floor when the rest of the campus was at the big football game. It was a Saturday afternoon and she had been left in charge of the college library where she worked. Except for Manny and her, the library was empty. They didn't go to the game because they had choir rehearsal after she got off work. Manny was keeping her company at the front desk till she closed up at four.

There alone they started fooling around in the stacks and the next thing they knew they were passionately kissing, with his hands exploring her and her hands exploring him. It's hard to say who kissed whom first. It just happened. Those two young Christian students, from a religion where sex before marriage was a cardinal sin, stood there necking and squirming with desire. Then amid all the religious books and Bibles, they began tearing at each other's clothes like they had gone mad. Indeed they had gone mad, because although there was nobody else there, the library was still opened to the public, with both doors wide open. The next thing they knew, they were down on the floor, going at it like animals in heat, with young Viola moaning from the pleasuring. She felt such new and wonderful sensations that she had to fight herself to keep from screaming out deliriously.

When Manny rolled off her, still in a daze she looked around for her panties. She retrieved them but was too weak to put them on. With her young body still on fire, she wanted only to lie there for a few more minutes and relish what she was feeling. To enjoy her maiden sex. Suddenly to her utter horror she realized what they had just done. "Oh Manny! What have we done!" she gasped. Bewildered she looked over at Emanuel lying there next to her with his trousers off, struggling to stay awake. How did she get in such an awful predicament? she wondered. Then to even greater horror, she realized where they were.

She leaped to her feet.

"Manny, we must never do that again. Remember, we're only good friends. Do you understand? You must promise," she said to him with tears in her eyes as they put on their clothes. He agreed.

That afternoon they had been very lucky, because except for a girl who unbeknownst to them dashed in and right back out after leaving some books on the check-in desk, no one else came into the library while they were making love. The girl returning the books didn't know they were back in the stacks.

On their way to the dormitory that afternoon, they both promised to get down on their knees when they got home and ask God to forgive them. That night when again down on her knees asking for forgiveness, young Viola Flowers promised God that she would be prepared for the Devil if he ever came at her from that direction again. For a few weeks she and Manny returned to being only good platonic friends, successfully fighting the physical attraction they had for each other.

In the end, though, the mutual passion was just too strong, and they were sucked back into sin again. They became torrid lovers again, making passionate love nearly every day, sometimes twice a day, for the next two and a half years. They often studied together in the dorm while lying in bed together on top of the covers, reading their textbooks, usually when cramming for some exam. Around break time from their studying, Viola would start sexually teasing Manny by rubbing her bare leg against his leg whenever she moved to adjust her pillow or to get more comfortable on top of the comforter.

It was particularly arousing for Manny when Viola did that while pretending to be still reading her Bible. It would drive him crazy with desire. She enjoyed being sexually wicked like that, which excited him all the more. She would wear that devilish smile she always wore when being naughty. She would then take his hand and place it gently on one of her breasts. He would put down his book and begin kissing her, his thing big and hard again, and then they would make passionate love. Afterwards they would go back to hitting the books as if nothing had happened.

She fell madly in love with Manny, and he with her. They became engaged to be married, which she hoped would make all the sex they were having less objectionable in the eyes of God.

This was why their breakup was so tragic.

****

Rev. Flowers best friend from childhood was Betty Harris who now lived in St. Louis, Missouri. Since Betty moved away when they were in junior high, the two of them stayed in close touch, often talking for hours on the telephone, which irked Manny Scott to no end when they were in college. "You two live on that damn phone," he would fuss whenever he visited Viola at her dorm and found her on the phone talking long-distance to Betty. Manny and Betty didn't like each other.

"Please watch your language, Manny. Don't use the Lord's name in vain. Betty and I are not on the telephone all the time. Betty had an important problem she needed to talk to me about," Viola would reply.

"Miss Gabby always has important problems she needs to talk about," he would retort sarcastically.

Once he overheard Viola discussing with Betty intimate details of his and Viola's relationship. Some of it sexual. Intimate little things about him. He was furious! What he heard left him speechless. Wasn't there anything sacred to her? Manny wondered about Viola. "How could you tell Betty all that personal stuff about us," he roared at her like a wounded lion. It was like he had been the victim of a monumental betrayal.

"What personal stuff? We were just sharing experiences as we've always done since we were kids. She's my best friends, remember," Viola replied nonchalantly, as if not understanding what all the fuss was about. To her it was simply a case of Betty and her sharing things of importance, something best friends do as best friends.

She and Manny had had that conversation a thousand times. It was their main source of friction and they argued about it endlessly. Trying to make him understand was like talking to a brick wall. Nothing got through.

"Don't you have a best friend that you tell important things to?" she asked him the first time they had that argument.

"I have many good friends I talk to about things, but never about the personal things that happen between you and me. That's private. That should be just between us."

"I don't mean just any good friend, Manny. I mean your best friend like Raymond. Do you ever talk to Raymond about your personal problems?"

"Of course I do. Ray and I talk all the times," he said defensively.

"I don't mean sports and male things like that. I mean, do you two ever talk about things bothering you deep down inside." She was speaking of how Manny would sometimes return to campus after a trip home very upset with his father. He and his father fought a lot.

"I could kill him! I could kill him!" he exclaimed to her once after just returning from home after a Christmas break, his voice rising in rage. "We were all having such a good time Christmas day, especially Ma. She loved the gifts we had gotten her. Then he had to spoil things with all his gloom and damnation. Why does he always have to piss on everything? He complained about everything. The gifts. The friends who came over. The neighbors who dropped by. The choral singing. Even Christmas dinner. Ma worked hard preparing that big meal, and all he could do was to find fault with it. I wanted to shove that bowl of cranberry sauce in his stupid face. He had Ma in tears. That man's the most negative person on earth. It seems to pain him to say anything nice about anyone. Nothing's ever fun when he's around. He always finds ways to spoil things."

This was typical of the kinds of grievances Manny would voice against his father every time he returned from home. Sometimes he would be nearly in tears. Viola would have to baby him for awhile until he calmed down. She always wondered if he ever told those disconcerting things to Raymond, his best friend. To her, those were the kinds of matters that one should discuss with one's best friend.

"Manny, do you ever talk to Raymond about how you really feel about your father? About how you sometimes wished he was dead?" she asked him one day.

"Of course not!" Manny intoned indignantly.

"But he's your best friend," she said puzzled.

"So what," he replied annoyed, not wanting to discuss it any further.

Her question was so outrageous to him that he became angrier. Of course he hadn't told Ray (or any of his other male friends, for that matter). What real man would ever tell another man something that personal about himself. Just thinking about telling Raymond made him tremble. True, he had told Viola, but that was different; they were lovers. It was okay to tell your lover about such things, but not the guys. What he had told her, and only her, was not to be repeated to anyone. He felt such confessions should be wrapped up and protected by their love. For the life of him he couldn't understand how females could be so carefree about blabbing about the intimate things in their lives to their so-called best friends.

Manny's father, a ranking minister in the Church of God in Christ, was a man Manny loved and hated at the same time. A man he admired and despised in the same breath. Viola found this very confusing. Manny's relationship with his father was much like her father's relationship with his father. Her grandfather. Just as she and Manny were the children of preachers, both of their fathers were sons of gospel ministers. Her grandfather and Manny's grandfather were important figures in the black holiness movement. Both men were instrumental in the splitting off of their respective churches from their mother churches. Thus like dissidents down through history, both men were strong, determined, doctrinaire, and very critical. Being fundamentalist preachers, both were very hard on their own children, from whom they expected circumspect behavior as children of pastors, and generally they were much harder on their sons than their daughters. Aunt Belle used to say that her big brother was so harsh on Viola's father that it often approached child abuse.

"Poor Tom Junior," she would opine sadly, "Tom Senior abused him so terribly that I sometimes ran into my room and cried." One day she told Viola, "The way Tom Senior treated your father was a shame. In our church people stupidly believe that Man's inherently bad, and that only the fear of God can keep him in line. And that it's the pastor's job to put that fear of God in the congregation. I believe religion should be much more than that. That's why when Mama died I got the hell out of there and moved back down South, where I became a Methodist, a church that allows a person room to breathe."

Viola believed Aunt Belle was too hard on the Church of God & Spirit.

When Manny returned to campus moody and upset with his father, Viola would pray that he and his father would someday make peace. "Your father's wrong for being so hard on you, Manny. But you must make space in your heart for your father's weakness. You must fill that space with compassion. That's the Christian way," she told Manny back in their Bible college days.

Manny promised himself that he would be a different kind of preacher than his father when he graduated, vowing to preach love and hope, not just hell and damnation.

Viola met Manny's father several times when she and Manny were dating. Except for his ever-present gloominess, she found him pleasant enough. Despite his severe theological views (even she grated at their razor-wire hardness), Manny's father was always nice to her. He seemed to respect her as a theological student aspiring to enter the ministry. He was proud of how well she was doing in school, and told her that he believed she would make a fine preacher. He thanked her for helping his son with his studies.

"I think your father's very nice," she would say to Manny whenever she thought he was being too critical of his dad, which was quite often since he blamed his father for all the rotten things in his life. A few times early in his youth Manny came dangerously close to getting into trouble with the law, all just to get back at his father.

"You just don't know my father," he would reply sourly.

Her discussions with Manny's father gave her some insight into the doctrinal struggles that her grandfather had years ago with

Manny's grandfather's wing of the Church of God in Christ. She remembered the stories her father used to tell about why their church split off from the Church of God in Christ, with her grandfather being the main leader in the revolt. In her mind she could visualize her grandfather and Manny's grandfather locking horns over theology like two mighty bulls. Two powerful snorting bulls pounding and goring each other bloodily until one of them turns and runs or falls dead in the struggle.

It was strange how differently those two great men had affected their own sons, both of whom went on to become top religious leaders in their own right. Her father became a gentle, poet-like minister, while Manny's father became a man of unceasing fire and brimstone. Both men were powerful religious leaders. In many ways Manny's father reminded her very much of her grandfather.

****

It was Manny's philandering that caused Viola to call off their engagement. An attractive woman couldn't pass him without him turning his head and following her with his eyes. And whenever Viola complained to him about it, he would maintain it was innocent. "What harm is there in only looking? You're always telling me that I should take more time to smell the roses," he would say, grinning like a Cheshire cat.

"She wasn't a rose," Viola would snap back, "She was a little hussy whose dress was not only too tight but too short. And it's not innocent, because where the eyes go, the body isn't far behind." At some point Manny's body started following his eyes, and he cheated on Viola more times than she cared to remember.

When they finally broke up, they were just getting started as ministers. It was a pity, for they made a great couple. She was so idealistic and optimistic, while he was so charismatic and powerful in his personality. They had planned to work together to make the world a better place. They both opposed war and injustice. Their preaching styles complemented each other's, and their singing voices blended well together. In religious musical numbers their big voices could be heard above the other singers, mixing like a well-rehearsed gospel duet. Most important, their bodies blended well together, mixing like chocolate syrup over caramel ice-cream.

Just thinking about how beautifully their bodies blended still caused shivers to shoot up Rev. Flowers' spine.

Despite their breakup years ago, they remained good friends.

Chapter Ten

Back in Georgia in 1910, the sheriff was determined to solve
the "Pine Cabin Killings," as the newspapers called the murders.
The sheriff sat across the table from Melvin Jenkins who was
being held for questioning about the murders. The deputy stood by
the office door and looked on. That was how they always
positioned themselves, good cop, bad cop, when interrogating
witnesses in the sheriff's office.

"You got yourself into some real trouble this time, Melvin," the
sheriff said to the young Negro man.

"I told you sheriff that I don't know nothing about them
murders," Melvin pleaded, greatly puzzled why the sheriff was still
holding him. The sheriff knew he wasn't a violent person and
didn't commit those murders, because the sheriff knew him when
he was a small boy and used to tag along with his bootlegging
father. Nor did they have anything else on him, for he was
confident they didn't find his whiskey stills. They could search
those woods for a million years and still wouldn't find them.

"That was your cabin, boy. What was your cousin Alphonso
doing out there with that strange woman?" the sheriff said as he
watched Melvin hungrily eye the bag of tobacco and cigarette
paper on the table in front of them. But he refused to offer him a
smoke. Seeing that also, out of pure spite, the deputy rolled and lit
up a cigarette and blew tobacco smoke in Melvin's direction.

"I already told you. She wasn't from around here. She was
married and was sneaking around on her husband. That's why they
were using my cabin."

The fat sheriff got to his feet and slowly walked around behind
the nervous young Negro.

"Who's Alphonso's poppa, boy? Don't you lie to me!" he
blurted out like someone on a bullhorn, almost busting Melvin's
eardrums, nearly frightening poor Melvin Jenkins out of his shoes.
The deputy snickered. The sheriff's fleshy white face was now
crimson.

This seemingly simple question jarred Melvin terribly; it made him sit up straight in his chair. Usually when asked by black folks of other black folks, this kind of question is considered benign and akin to asking someone about his or her family, such as: "I think I know your poppa, boy. How's he doing?" It's a question particularly important to older black people in the neighborhood because it allows them to follow the genes in their community from generation to generation.

"Boy, aren't you Herbert Taylor's son?" some old man might ask you because of how you walk or how you cock your head when you laugh. Years ago the old man had buddied around with Herbie Taylor. They went fishing together and hung out together at the pool hall. In fact, he and Herbie Taylor were once in love with the same girl who spurned both of them and ended up marrying someone else. The old man is right. You are related to Herbert Taylor, but you're his grandson, not his son. The old man then scratches his head, befuddled by how fast times flies.

You can see, therefore, that for black folks it's a question about community and the DNA in that community. Thus for a black person when asked by another black person, the question is usually friendly.

It's a totally different story, however, when the questioner is a white person, especially a white lawman. Many a black father, uncle or cousin has ended up on a chain gang or even dead because someone answered that innocent-sounding question. The question: "Who's your poppa, boy?" from the lips of a white man, particularly a white man with a badge, seldom meant anything good for the black community. Melvin knew this from personal experience. The first time his bootlegging father was arrested was when he, Melvin as a small boy, truthfully answered that question from federal law officers. Tears flowed down his young face when those white men later took his father away in handcuffs. Melvin had violated the cardinal rule of the black community about not willy-nilly giving information to strange white people.

But in his present predicament Melvin knew he had to answer the sheriff's questions truthfully. Possible murder charges were hanging over his head. "Alphonso's poppa is named Alphonso too. He plays in a band in Memphis," Melvin stammered weakly.

There were many in the black community, including Melvin's family, who believed that Alphonso's father was a light-skinned

Negro banjo player, not a white man as some gossip had it. The banjo player had lived in town briefly before moving on to Memphis after getting Alphonso's then teenage mother pregnant. They say that was why she eventually took the kid and moved to Memphis also.

The sheriff could see that Melvin Jenkins was probably telling the truth. He knew that many in the black section of town held that view about Alphonso's paternity. So he returned to his first line of questioning.

"Who was the dead woman?" he asked Melvin again; in fact it was the hundredth time he had put that question to Melvin.

"Like I told you, I don't know. All I know is that she lived in another county. Alphonso went there every Sunday to see her."

"What's her name?"

"I already told you."

"Well tell me again, boy."

"Alphonso called her 'Buttercup.' That's all I know."

The deputy let go a big laugh as he did when Melvin answered that question on other occasions.

"Buttercup? I know you niggers have strange names, but that's a new one," the sheriff remarked like he had heard that name for the first time.

"I don't think that's her real name. Alphonso just called her that," Melvin said once again in a dry raspy voice.

He was still dying for a cigarette. Furthermore, the straight back chair was killing his back. There was a glass of water in front of him but he was afraid to touch it. His hands were shaking too much for him to get the glass to his lips without spilling it. It was important that he stayed calm. His father had warned him that when apprehended by the law to say as little as possible. "Lawmen will take what you say and twist it around and use it against you at trial," his father had told him.

"What's her real name?" the sheriff asked Melvin Jenkins again.

"I don't know. Wasn't her real name in that little Bible of hers?"

"What little Bible?" the sheriff's eyes lit up like lanterns.

"She always carried a little Bible around with her."

"You mean a prayer book?" The sheriff's eyes widened even

more.

"Is that what you call it? Yeah. She carried it with her wherever she went. I never saw her without it."

The sheriff looked at his deputy suspiciously.

****

When the deputy returned from taking Melvin Jenkins back to his cell, the sheriff asked him sharply, "Did you take that prayer book from the cabin?"

"Aw c'mon, Chief. You know I wouldn't do anything like that." The deputy's face turned a little red since he and the sheriff often took little things they wanted from crime scenes. The sheriff, of course, always got the first divvy, and they never pocketed anything that had evidentiary value.

"Did you see it?" the sheriff asked with narrowed eyes.

"I searched that cabin thoroughly. There was no prayer book. Honest, Chief," the deputy said nervously.

"Hmm," the fat sheriff groaned skeptically as he scratched his stubbly chin.

****

The sheriff decided to investigate where those expensive women's clothes found in the cabin came from. He would start with ascertaining the store where they were bought. Perhaps if he learned that, then maybe he could identify the dead woman. Even though he doubted that the clothes were purchased locally, he started with the merchants in town.

"Did any of these things come from here, Hank?" the sheriff asked Henry Hinkley, the proprietor of Hinkley's Dry Goods Store down the street. The dead woman's clothes were of a finer quality than normally worn by women living in their neck of the woods, especially black women. He showed the shopkeeper the expensive dress, stockings, and shoes from the cabin. He hoped the shopkeeper might have some idea where they had been purchased.

"These are too highfalutin to have been bought around here," Hank Hinkley said after examining the exquisite material, the elegant stitching, and the fashionable design of the garments.

"They probably came from Macon or Atlanta," he ventured a guess.

Taking the clothes and shoes with him in a bag, the sheriff traveled to Macon to make inquiries at upscale stores there. Among other things, Macon was the home of Wesleyan College for Women and Mercer University. After visiting several downtown stores in Macon without any success, one store manager suggested Keeson's. "Try Keeson's. Many of the rich college girls shop there," he told the sheriff. Keeson's had been mentioned at several of the other stores that the sheriff had visited as places that might carry that price dress and shoes. Hence the sheriff carried his murder investigation to Keeson's Women Clothiers located next door to Orenstein's, Macon's most fashionable jewelry store.

"We don't carry that brand of shoes, but yes that's our dress," the sales manager at Keeson's told the sheriff after checking the label on the dress, "This was our most popular item in last fall's line of dresses. That dress sold out the very first day we put it on display, which was rather surprising considering it was much pricier than what we usually carry."

He added proudly, "I do the buying for the store. I remember that dress well. There were several dozens of them in different colors and sizes. The salesman we bought them from said we were the only store outside of New York City and Chicago that had that dress. I think that's why they sold out so fast. They were all gone in a matter of hours. It isn't everyday that women can find something here in Macon that they can't get in Atlanta."

"Do you have many colored customers?" the sheriff asked him.

"We don't sell to Negroes in this store," the man said snootily.

Hearing that, the thing that popped into the sheriff's head was that the nigger girl might have worked for a wealthy white family who gave her the dress. Maybe the white woman discovered when she got home that it didn't fit properly and gave it to her maid. Maybe she disliked the color or found the design a little too daring. There were a thousand reasons why she might've given the dress to her Negro help, the sheriff figured.

It irked him deeply that rich white families were always giving nice things away to the niggers who worked for them. Clothes, shoes, leftover food, furniture. It angered him the way niggers dressed up on Sundays in those hand-me-down clothes, and strutted around at church like they owned the world.

He had in mind August Perkins, a big shot deacon in the local Negro Baptist Church, and the way he strutted around town on Sundays fondling that big gold watch of his on the gold chain that draped cheekily from the buttons of his suit vest. The watch was left to him by his father who had worked on the railroad until his death. The fine clothes Deacon Perkins always wore on Sundays, however, came from his sister in Atlanta, who got them from a wealthy white family she worked for in suburban Atlanta. Instead of donating their old clothes to the Salvation Army, the rich white family gave them to Deacon Perkins' sister, their maid, who mailed them to her relatives, the Perkins family. Most of the time the clothes were like new and sometimes the expensive shoes were barely used.

"Why don't rich white people take the time and give the nice things they no longer want to poor whites who could use them as well?" the sheriff cursed to himself. Everything always went to the darkies. He thought of how shabbily his sister's family dressed on those rare occasions when they went to church. He thought of how shabbily his nieces and nephews dressed when they went to school, sometimes with patches on their clothes and hole in their shoes. Sometimes with dried snot on their little faces. The thought made the sheriff's blood boil.

"This dress belonged to a young colored woman. Do you have any idea how she got it?" he asked Keeson's sales manager next.

"She probably stole those clothes. Colored people are always stealing things. That's why we don't allow them in this store," he replied smugly.

****

A few days later the sheriff sat at his desk going through some files. He was still looking for leads in the case. He packed a fresh plug of chewing tobacco into one side of his mouth, which made him look like someone with a bad toothache. The cabin murders had consumed him totally. Unsolved crimes bothered him to no end. He was a very conscientious sheriff, and a fairly incorruptible peace officer, who had won reelection seven times.

True, he and his deputy sometimes appropriated for themselves small things from crime scenes, but never anything really needed at trial. Also never anything of any real value. As a rule they only took small things, usually articles having meager value or something the criminal had no business with in the first place. Again, never anything with evidentiary value.

The sheriff figured the things he and his deputy sometimes took were small recompense for their low salaries that the County Board of Commissioners hadn't increased in years. But when something of real value was involved, he would make his deputy keep his hands off of it, and take it into protective custody. The deputy didn't even have to ask. He would look over and see that "Don't-you-dare-take-that" expression on the sheriff's face, and leave it alone. Like, for instance, the time when the rich lady who slit her wrists died in her bathtub. In their investigation of the suicide, they came across a six-carat diamond ring on the glass shelf in the woman's bathroom. They could have easily pocketed the valuable ring without anyone ever knowing, since she lived alone. It wasn't needed for evidence or anything. Instead, until he could turn it over to the proper next of kin, the sheriff kept it in his office safe, along with the woman's other valuables that were lying around her home unprotected.

Or like when some bootleggers escaped from one of the sheriff's raids and left a bag of money behind in their haste to flee. Had it been only a few dollars, he and his deputy probably would have divided the money between them. But because there was nearly a thousand dollars in that bag, the sheriff took it and locked it in his safe for safekeeping, even though the money would eventually end up being escheated to the county government.

The sheriff was very discouraged about the way the investigation was going. He still hadn't learned the identity of the murdered woman. He was certain that she wasn't from his county. Even his snitches in the Negro section of town were of no help. He made some inquiries in a few neighboring counties, but came up with nothing. No one had been reported missing.

Although there were no fingerprints on file for either of the victims, he had identified the male victim to his satisfaction. The man was Alphonso Baker, a young black man who used to live in town before he moved to Memphis as a child with his mother. The sheriff knew the Baker family well. It was a large Negro family in town with plenty of lazy boys who were always getting into trouble with the law. A few he had personally sent to prison. The Baker family had kin all over Georgia. Alphonso's mother was the youngest of the Baker girls. She used to be seen back then swishing that cute little black ass of hers around in the Negro section of town, giving everybody a hard-on. One of the town rumors was that Alphonso Baker's illegitimate father was an important white man whose identity was unknown. There might have been some truth to that rumor since Alphonso was very light-complected. Then again, maybe not. Negroes come in such strange colors, the sheriff thought. Bud, the big burly Negro who worked at the granary, came to mind. Bud had nappy light brown hair and a pinkish white face covered with big brown freckles, yet his nigger parents were black as coal.

The sheriff's mind toggled between the important white man and the Negro banjo player as possibly being Alphonso's father.

Thinking back, the sheriff surmised that he might have met Alphonso Baker once when the latter was a teenager. He remembered investigating a report some years ago that some colored boys were shooting pigeons atop the high school building. Even though against the law, boys of both races hunted pigeons at the white high school all the time. While the pigeons roosted at night under the eaves, the boys would scale the outside of the high school building with flashlights, climb up to the roof, then lower themselves down under the eaves where the pigeons were sleeping. They would catch the birds by blinding them with their flashlights. The boy down under the eaves would hand the pigeons up to his buddies on the roof where the birds were placed into sacks and taken home to be eaten or sold.

The boys caught pigeons mostly for the thrill of the climb. However, after the Simmons kid fell a few years ago and was paralyzed for life, the sheriff and his deputy tried hard to keep the boys off the dangerous school rooftop, particularly the black boys who had no busy being in the neighborhood.

Anyway, one Saturday afternoon the sheriff got a call that two Negro boys were at the high school shooting pigeons with a .22 rifle. When he and his deputy arrived at the school they found Melvin Jenkins and another boy a little younger hunting pigeons with a BB gun that had been mistaken for a rifle. Having arrested

Melvin's father many times for suspicion of bootlegging, the sheriff knew Melvin Jenkins well. But neither he nor his deputy knew the younger boy. At the time Melvin said the boy was his cousin. Was that boy Alphonso Baker? Maybe not. All niggers looked like cousins. He couldn't remember the face of the other boy, save he was light colored. That was some years ago.

He didn't arrest the colored boys that day at the high school. He just took their BB gun away from them, and warned them to leave the pigeons alone. He also warned them to stay on their own side of town. He later gave the air rifle to his young nephew, since the niggers had probably stolen it anyway.

Chapter Eleven

The dead woman's expensive clothes troubled the sheriff deeply. He didn't believe she stole them. They were probably given to her by a man. She was pretty enough. Therefore, he and his deputy sat down in the office one afternoon and raked their brains and compiled a list of men who could have possibly bought those costly clothes. The list was short since there weren't many black men in the county with that kind of money. The list even included a few white men with reputations for cavorting with Negro women.

"What about Frank, Chief?" the deputy asked warily.

"You mean Frank Diggs?" the sheriff replied grimly. Frank Diggs had occurred to him as well, but he quickly dismissed the idea as being preposterous. It was true that in his youth, Diggs, a white man, was known for liking his coffee black. But murder?

"Yes. Frank's rumored to be Alphonso Barker's daddy. At least there're many niggers who think so. You know that," the deputy said.

Frank Diggs was their state senator who was running for the U.S. Senate. The senator had been very wild in his college days, during which time he acquired a fondness for black pussy, at least according to the rumors. His old college reputation as a "nigger lover" nearly cost him his first election. His wealthy father had to spend a ton of money hushing things up.

The sheriff gave his deputy a look. Yes, he did know that. Somehow the old rumor that in his college days Frank Diggs knocked up the cute Baker girl had slipped his mind.

"Nah," he finally said to his deputy as he decided not to add Diggs' name to their list. "The notion's too absurd," he grunted to his deputy.

****

When his deputy left, the sheriff sat there alone at his desk in anguish. No matter how hard he tried, he couldn't get Frank Diggs off his mind. The rumor that Diggs was Alphonso's father gnawed at him like a dog chewing a bone. If the rumor was true, it might explain the murders.

He recalled that he recently received some campaign literature from Senator Diggs. So he opened the bottom drawer of his desk and fished through all the stuff he had dropped in there to be sorted through later. He found one of Frank Diggs' election leaflet that contained a good picture of him. He studied Frank Diggs' photo carefully. Those piercing blue eyes that had made the state senator so popular with the ladies before he married into one of the wealthiest families in the South. That engaging smile that had won him every election he ran in since returning to Georgia after law school. It was a smile he hoped would carry him all the way to the U.S. Senate. Next there were those bushy eyebrows that ran in the Diggs family, going back to Frank Diggs' granddaddy, who once owned the largest cotton plantation and the most slaves in that part of Georgia.

"Is Frank that nigger's daddy?" the sheriff wondered aloud, chewing his tobacco like an old cow chewing its cud. "Maybe young Baker returned to town with his girl friend to blackmail Frank. Maybe he'd been putting the squeeze on Frank all along. That might explain the expensive clothes the girl was wearing. Maybe those clothes were bought with Frank's money."

He spit a wad of tobacco juice into the spittoon, again not missing. "Would that be motive enough for Frank to kill them?" he kept asking himself about the jigsaw puzzle he was trying to solve. Yes it would, was his painful conclusion. "In the wrong hands, that kind of information could ruin a white politician's career," he said to himself aloud.

In his policeman's mind, it explained all the hatred that seemed to underlie those awful murders. He knew that Frank Diggs was a mean sonofabitch when he was young. He recalled all the stories that used to be told about him. When in college Diggs used to boast about all the girls he had screwed, including Negro girls.

He looked at Diggs' photo again and rubbed his chin, his eyes fastened on Frank's bushy eyebrows. He recalled how Fred the barber used to tell the guys in the barbershop about how sensitive Frank Diggs was about his bushy eyebrows. "Most men who come in here are particular about their sideburns or mustaches. Some customers worry about me taking too much off the top. But not young Frank Diggs. With him the big thing are his eyebrows. He won't get out of the barber chair until I trim them down just right. His eyebrows grow like thick weeds. He blames his daddy and granddaddy for passing those eyebrows down to him and ruining his otherwise handsome face," Fred used to chuckle to the guys in the barbershop. The sheriff had personally heard those remarks himself.

"If Frank Diggs is Alphonso Baker's daddy, then maybe that nigger inherited those same thick eyebrows," he wondered to himself. "Negroes aren't generally known for having bushy eyebrows."

He got to his feet and lumbered over to the filing cabinet to look at the photographs of the dead bodies. But they couldn't help him. The shotgun blasts had blown away too much of Alphonso's face.

He put the bulky file back into the filing cabinet, shut the drawer, and walked back to his desk. The more he thought about it, the more convinced he became that Frank Diggs was a legitimate suspect. Frank was a mean sonofabitch, going way back, he reminded himself again. And he could personally testify to that.

The sheriff and Frank Diggs grew up together in the same small town, but on different sides of the railroad tracks. Their lives were vastly different. In his youth Frank Diggs attended expensive private schools where he got a good education, while the sheriff attended a small rundown one-room country school where he was barely taught to read and write. The sheriff's school was so poor that his teachers (all white) sometimes had to borrow teaching supplies and materials from the colored school down the road (all Negro) that was also very poor.

Conversely, often the Negro teachers borrowed books and supplies from his white school. Both schools had been woefully neglected by the local school board, which seemed not to care whether the poor white children and black children were educated or not. In his opinion, his poor white school was treated almost as badly as the black schools in the district. He hated being treated like a white nigger just because he was dirt poor. It were as if the county didn't want to waste good taxpayers' money on educating them since they were destined for a life of backbreaking work as field hands.

Once during a long rainy spell his school house sprung leaks that were so bad that the white children couldn't use the building. By special arrangement with the black teachers at the black school, the white pupils shared classes with the black students for several weeks until the rains stopped and their building was repaired. This might have been the first instance of racially integrated classes in Georgia history. Of course, it was done without the knowledge of the all-white school board. Race mixing was against the law.

Furthermore, it was a very dangerous thing for those Negro and white teachers to do, because many white families in the district belonged to the Ku Klux Khan. There would have been serious trouble had the Khan gotten wind of what the teachers did. Yet at great risk to their careers, if not their lives, the teachers did it for the welfare of the children. Because many of the children were playmates outside of school, there was no trouble in the integrated classes.

The sheriff's father, a small dirt farmer who eventually lost his farm to the bank, hated the big white farmers and plantation owners even more than he hated Negroes. His father never joined the Khan because the local Khan leader was a wealthy farmer who evicted him and his family one winter from the farm they were sharecropping for the Khan leader. The dispute was over a $5 grocery bill at the Khan leader's company store. As a consequence, not only did the sheriff's father not join the Klan, he didn't allow his sons to join either. The sheriff was only nine-years-old at the time, and he grew up also hating the Klan.

Frank Diggs continued on to Vanderbilt and then to law school, while the sheriff had to get a job at a garage that repaired heavy farm equipment, buggies, wagons, and a few horseless carriages in use at the time. This was the tail end of the horse-and-buggy era.

"Frank Diggs was a mean sonofabitch in those days," the sheriff mumbled to himself again as he remembered the night years ago when Frank's car limped with engine trouble into the repair shop where the sheriff worked. This was before the sheriff became a lawman. That night Frank was driving his father's new Buick, which was from the first batch of Buicks built in Flint.

When Frank Diggs pulled into the garage, there was a pretty blonde college girl beside him in the front seat. "If you don't shut up, I'll smack you again!" the sheriff, when under the hood working on Frank Diggs' engine, heard Frank curse. Then when cleaning the windshield, he saw the girl hunkered down in the front seat with a black eye, a busted lip, and her clothes hanging in shreds from her trim white shoulders. She was whimpering from fear. He didn't recognize her, but he was sure she wasn't from around there. She was probably a student from the women's college in the next county. She and Frank had probably just left the Diggs plantation. Frank's parents weren't at home, and everyone in town knew they were traveling in Europe at the time.

Diggs quickly paid him that night and sped away. As Diggs' motorcar faded in the distance, it dawned on him that Diggs had probably raped that girl. He didn't report it to the authorities, because knowing how the law worked in that neck of the woods, the powerful Diggs family might have ended up pinning the rape on him, a poor white boy. That was the night when he vowed to run for sheriff someday.

Upon returning home from law school, Frank Diggs worked awhile in the district attorney's office before running for the state legislature. Meanwhile, over on his side of town, the sheriff worked awhile in a low-level position in the county's road department. Then he ran for office three times before finally winning and becoming the sheriff. It was miraculous that he got elected, considering that he was the first person in the county's history to become sheriff without a Ku Klux Khan endorsement.

"Back then he was a mean bastard!" the sheriff repeated under his breath, referring to Frank Diggs.

He examined State Senator Diggs' photo again. Frank Diggs was a respectable church-going married man. Was Alphonso his illegitimate son? Nah! The notion was too preposterous, he thought. "Niggers are always speculating about some white man being some nigger's daddy," he growled under his breath. In fact, he had been the butt of a few such rumors himself.

He threw the political leaflet back into his desk drawer. Frank Diggs' blue eyes and bushy eyebrows looked up at him as if to thank him. He closed the drawer. "A nigger killed those niggers. I just know it. Niggers are always killing each other," he scoffed aloud.

Then he changed his mind and reopened the drawer and

retrieved the leaflet. "Just in case, I better go over to Clarksville and have a talk with Frank," he told himself when his sense of duty got the best of him.

The sheriff got to his feet. "Egad!" he gulped when an imaginary newspaper headline flashed in his mind: *Beloved Politician Murders Negro Son*. It made him stopped in his tracks. Then he mustered his courage and reached for his hat. Spitting a big wad of tobacco and scoring another bull's eye, he shook his head sadly and went out the door.

Chapter Twelve

Los Angeles in 2000. An important factor in Rev. Flowers' decision to buy the white church some years ago was that the church building and the parsonage next door were on separate parcels of land, which enabled her and Albert to personally own the house that served as the parsonage, while the Church of God & Spirit owned the church edifice and grounds.

She was also very impressed by the large, modern stainless steel kitchen and dining hall that the white parishioners built just before they decided to sell the church. The new kitchen was what largely persuaded Rev. Flowers and her board of trustees to buy the property. They saw it as perfect for the soup kitchen they had dreamed of operating: a program with a fulltime cook so they could provide hot meals for the poor and meals-on-wheels for the sick and elderly in their community.

After they moved into their new church, the first thing Rev. Flowers did was to hire Beulah as the cook, who was still with them today.

A few years ago a young white man started dropping newspapers off at the church on a regular basis without obtaining Rev. Flowers' permission to do so, leaving a stack in the vestibule of the church and another stack in the dining hall for the diners to read. The newspapers were free. Paul Sweeny was a gregarious young man with plenty on his mind. A community activist always in a T-shirt and sandals, he was from the Catholic World Workers Party that published the throw-away newspaper.

Rev. Flowers found the publication unsuitable for the vestibule of the church, but she did allow Paul Sweeny, with Beulah's approval, to leave a stack of them every week in the church mess hall. Even though the newspapers was objectionable for church members, whose religion generally required them to remain apart from matters of the secular world, especially politics and international affairs, Rev. Flowers reasoned that the newspapers were OK for the homeless people who came in everyday for meals. Besides, she liked the young Catholic, and was intrigued by his brand of revolutionary Catholicism.

If she was in her office, Paul would deliver Rev. Flowers her copy personally. Like with the Awake! magazine that the Jehovah's Witnesses handed out, she looked forward to the Catholic newspaper every week because it contained much information not found elsewhere that she found very interesting, particularly the articles on Africa. Much of her enjoyment came from reading materials that she really wasn't supposed to be reading as pastor of a gospel church. To her there was something deliciously sinful about sitting alone in her office in the quiet of the afternoon reading such secular material.

It was Paul's newspaper, for instance, that opened her eyes to much of what was happening in the larger world. It made her start asking herself serious questions about places like Latin America, Asia, and Africa. Most startling, she started seeking answers outside the Bible. The old answers that blamed everything on sin and evil didn't work for her anymore. She needed better answers to help her understand such horrendous events as the genocide of Africans by Africans in Rwanda, or Jews and Arabs shooting guns at each other in the Church of the Nativity in Bethlehem, the holy birth place of her savior Jesus Christ.

Sometimes Paul would sit down and chat with her, and on those occasions they never argued religion, but instead usually talked about all the injustice in the world. It was hard to believe that when they first met a few years ago, their relationship got off to a rocky start. In fact, at first she didn't like Paul Sweeny. Only a few minutes into their relationship they had a big fight, and she came close to throwing him out of her office.

Here's what happened. One day she said to him in good humor, "All the wickedness in the world can bring tears to your eyes, don't you agree?"

He replied smugly, "Yes, it does, but I doubt if you and I agree on what's wicked in this world."

"Oh? And what is 'wickedness' to you?" she asked him wryly, not knowing where he was going with that.

"Wickedness is our government's spending billions of dollars on armament to defend us from trumped-up enemies while our public schools and infrastructure fall apart because we claim we have no money. It's giving the wealthy big fat tax cuts while our citizens are forced to sleep on the streets because we say we can't afford to build them housing. It's giving corporate subsidies to large global corporations while our elderly can't afford their prescription drugs, and the working poor can't get decent medical care because they don't have health insurance. It's wanting to destroy a Social Security system that's the best in the world for some cockeyed Wall Street stock scheme. That's the wickedness we Christians should be concerned about, not with just saving people's souls and chasing pie-in-the-sky rewards," he replied with youthful arrogance.

Ouch! That hurt! Rev. Flowers took the remark as a personal affront. She felt like she had just been violently kicked in her shinbone. "How dare him! The young squirt! Who does he think he is, anyway!" she screamed to herself. Although she screamed in silence, fire shot from her eyes. He had struck a nerve. "Pie-in-the-sky, indeed," she hissed under her breath.

She decided then and there that she didn't like young Paul Sweeny. She knew there were other kinds of wickedness in the world, and she didn't need him to remind her of that. She saw Paul's remark as another instance of people disrespecting believers in evangelicalism. Was this how young Paul saw her church? Did he see them as just a group of crazy Bible thumpers chasing the devil all day long while voicing empty Biblical clichés? He had mentioned fundamentalists. What did that word really mean? Was she a fundamentalist? Didn't all Christians struggle with Scripture? Didn't they all struggle madly with the question of when the Bible was to be taken literally, or just taken figuratively?

Rev. Pat Robertson's famed radio ministry, the 700 Club, was usually held up as an example of fundamentalist preaching. True, she liked the preaching of many of the 700 Club ministers, but that didn't mean that she shared all their political views. And it was also true that there were people in her church who attributed all wrongdoing in the world to Satan. People who believed that all one had to do was believe in the Bible and then everything would be fine. There were many who cared only about the Second Coming, and not about the plight of human beings here on earth. But not all members of her church felt that way. She certainly didn't feel that way.

Her church was much more than about just saving souls, she

told young Paul harshly. She told him that she had many parishioners who cared about what was happening in the world. Brother Boyd years ago at great personal risk to himself helped get the union started at the Goodman Rubber plant, and had walked numerous picket lines. Though now retired, he still proudly wore his union button on his suit lapel every Sunday. And there was Sister Carol, a registered nurse, who served five years in Africa providing medical care to the poor, and returned to the United States only when she herself caught malaria.

Young Paul Sweeny had mentioned "pie-in-the-sky." She didn't believe that "pie-in-the-sky" was what Jesus taught in the Bible. She believed he taught much more than that. Jesus wanted everyone to live lives filled with love and charity, so everybody could enjoy "pie-on-earth." The postulates of Matthews 6:10 were clear: "Thy kingdom come. Thy will be done on earth, as it is in heaven."

It was her belief that most black gospel folks read the Bible more figuratively, more imaginatively, more hopefully, than most white born-again Christians, who took their Bible more literally and more pessimistically.

Most of all, she didn't need a middle-class white boy barely dry behind the ears to lecture her on social injustice. She knew that people had to struggle to survive in life. She thought of the homeless children whose homeless parents brought them to church on Sundays. Before bringing them to church, their parents had tried to clean and dress them up the best they could, but the little guys still smelled of the gutter. Those children always brought tears to Rev. Flowers' eyes, for as hard as the church worked to find homes for them, the line for the homeless seemed endless and at times seemed like a losing battle.

But before she could give young Sweeny a piece of her mind that day, her presence was required in another part of the church, and when she returned to her office, he was gone. She was still hopping mad when she got back, and that was the afternoon when she denied him permission to leave his newspapers at the church. Had he not been such a smart aleck, she might have allowed the newspapers in the dining hall.

The next time Paul Sweeny stopped by the church, Rev. Flowers spoke to him bluntly about the last time he was there. It caught him by surprise because he hadn't realized he had offended her so. He apologized profusely. "I didn't mean it personally, Rev. Flowers. And I didn't mean just you. I meant that all churches should be more involved in fighting for world peace and social justice, including my own church. I criticize conservative Catholic priests about this all the time. I believe all Christians have a duty to stand up for what Jesus really stood for," he told her.

He then hung his head and said remorsefully, "I guess my remarks were kind of stupid, considering all the good work this church does feeding the homeless."

She appreciated his honesty and understood he had meant no harm that day, and it was only his youthful exuberance. So she forgave him. After allowing him to leave copies of his newspaper in the dining hall, she asked him, "By the way, Paul, what made you think my sympathies were with the rich and powerful?"

"Since you're a fundamentalist and a Republican, I just thought—" he stuttered. Not wanting to get into any more trouble with her, he didn't finish the sentence. Knowing that her husband palled around with conservative Republicans, he just presumed he knew her politics as well.

"Well, I'm not a Republican. I'm a Democrat," she replied sharply, "And if by fundamentalist you mean my evangelicalism, yes I am. I believe in a fairly strict reading of the Scripture. But don't assume just because you know my religion that you know my views on social issues. It's unfair, Paul. I didn't prejudge you just because you're Catholic."

"I'm sorry I prejudged you, Rev. Flowers. That was very unchristian of me. I shouldn't have done it."

"Just don't do it again. Now let's go to the dining hall and have a cup of coffee. You can tell me about the peace demonstration you just returned from," she said.

As two devout Christians with the same social views, she and Paul discovered that day that they could talk to each other about many things they really couldn't share with someone of their own faith. She enjoyed listening to Paul talk about his peace work with various peace groups around the country.

He was an admirer of the brothers Daniel and Philip Berrigan, the courageous Roman Catholic priests who had been arrested numerous times and served long stretches in prison for their peace activities. They were his heroes. He had gone on many peace actions with them. Like the Berrigan brothers, Paul too believed that Isaiah 2:4 of the Bible called for modern weaponry, like the swords of old, being beaten into plowshares.

Rev. Flowers admired how Paul stood up for what he believed in, and how he put his beliefs into action. "Those of us who have voices must speak up for the voiceless. That's called speaking truth to power," he would say to her grandly.

****

Paul was right that Rev. Flowers' husband Albert had changed his political affiliation from the Democratic Party to the Republican Party. "White liberals seem to resent black people making a little money, while Republicans don't," Albert told her that day when he decided to switch parties after believing in liberal politics all his life, including being an officer in his union. He liked the way Republicans supported entrepreneurship. Despite all of Albert's good arguments, Viola refused to join him in the switch. Even though she was pro-life, the Republicans had too many other policies that she opposed deeply.

Chapter Thirteen

A couple of years later, one morning after the homeless had finished their breakfast and left the church, and the janitor had cleaned up the church's dining hall, Rev. Flowers saw this solitary male figure hunkered over at a table in a far corner of the hall. He was wearing a hooded jacket, and at first glance she thought it was the white man who sometimes came around to trim their trees. She waved to him, but there was no response. Whoever it was, because there was no coffee mug in front of him, the man wasn't having his morning coffee. In ruffled slept-in clothes he appeared forlorn and hapless. Concerned that it might be a trespasser she went over to check.

Halfway over, she saw it was Paul Sweeny. "Good morning, Paul. I didn't recognize you sitting over here alone."

Paul didn't answer her. He just looked up at her and then resumed staring down vacantly at the surface of the table. He looked like someone who had just witnessed a little dog being squashed by a big truck. His young white face was twisted and colorless.

"Paul, what's wrong?" she asked, now worried; she had never seen him like that before, so deflated and wretched. Normally he was always very upbeat and ready to take on the world. Usually just being around him cheered her up, which was one of the main reasons she always enjoyed his company. Rev. Flowers' first thought was that Paul's mother, whom she knew he lived with, had died, because the last time they talked he had mentioned that his mother was seeing a doctor about severe pains in her chest.

Paul looked up at her with a pitiful expression on his face. "Do you mind if I sit here for awhile?" he finally spoke, sounding like a weary mourner who had just returned by foot from a distant burial.

"Of course you may." With her cup of coffee in hand she sat down across from him. "What's wrong?" she asked him again softly.

"They're destroying the church," he said after a long silence. He was nearly in tears.

She realized immediately what Paul was talking about. He was referring to the earthshaking scandal that had just shocked the world involving scores of Roman Catholic priests sexually molesting children of the church. Instead of reporting or firing the pedophilic priests when learning about them, some bishops merely transferred them to unsuspecting parishes where they continued to molest children. One priest, after being so transferred, sexually assaulted twenty-six more boys, raping one boy on a regular basis for nine years without being discovered. The scandal so outraged Catholic parishioners that the laity started demanding reforms, some calling for criminal charges being filed against the priests.

At first Rev. Flowers surmised that perhaps some priest had sexually abused Paul when he was an altar boy. The thought sent chills up her spine. Poor Paul! She recalled her little Catholic friend who lived around the corner from her when she was a small girl living in Iowa. She remembered how as children they used to compare their respective churches. Her little white friend used to joke about Violet's church being so small in comparison to her own large Catholic church with its beautiful stained glass windows, confession booths, and dark mysterious nooks and crannies everywhere. "Dark mysterious nooks and crannies? Was that where the priests took the children?" Viola Flowers asked herself sadly.

"Didn't you know, Paul?" she asked him.

He replied grimly, "At the newspaper we've known for years that the Church was having problems with pedophilic priests, but we had no idea until now that the problem was so deep and widespread. Not just the United States, but all over the world. Those damn perverts are everywhere. They're destroying the moral authority of the Church, and I blame the bishops and the cardinals." Paul's young face was like a slab of concrete, his words bitter.

He then said angrily, "Brave priests are risking their lives every day to help the poor in Latin America, and the Church won't lift a finger to help them. The bigwigs want no part of their revolutionary theology. Yet they're spending millions protecting sexual perverts. Giving them cushy jobs instead of sending them to jail. I'm so angry that I'm seriously thinking about leaving the Church. I just don't believe our clergy anymore. I'm ashamed to be a Catholic."

The brave priests Paul was talking about were the revolutionary priests in Latin America fighting alongside the landless and jobless against the rich property owners and businessmen and their paramilitary thugs.

Rev. Flowers reached across the table, took Paul's hands, and counseled him like he was one of her own flock, "Before you do anything rash, Paul, have a good long talk with God. Please. Tell him how you feel. Tell him that you're angry at the church, and ask him to help you with this anger. Ask him to help the church. Pray for the church."

"I suppose you're right. Thanks, Rev. Flowers," he said, feeling better.

When Rev. Flowers got to her feet to return to her office, he asked her wanly, "Do you mind if I hang around here for awhile? For some reason this is where I want to be at the moment. I can feel God here."

"Make yourself at home," she smiled.

"And I thought we had problems," she said to herself with gratitude as she left the dining hall, referring to her own small church.

Again she thought of her little Catholic friend back in her childhood. "Mysterious nooks and crannies? Was that where some priest took Paul?" she couldn't help thinking. Then she dismissed the notion as being absurd.

****

An hour later when she passed the kitchen, she saw Paul wearing an apron helping Beulah peel potatoes and he and Beulah were laughing about something. By the look on his young white face he appeared to have made his peace with God. Two hours later she saw him picking some peaches from the trees in the side yard so Beulah could make some pies.

The way Paul clung to Beulah's apron string all that afternoon made Rev. Flowers wonder again about Paul's altar boy days. She thought of the pedophilic priests. Was there more to Paul's story than he had told her? She hoped her fears were unfounded.

In any case, she was very pleased that the Church of God &

Spirit was there for Paul in his time of need.

Chapter Fourteen

Rev. Flowers was on her computer in her office finalizing her trip to the Midwest Conference in St. Louis. At first she considered staying with Betty Harris, an old girlfriend now living in St. Louis. Staying with Betty rather than in a hotel would help her limited travel budget, she figured. Staying in private homes during conferences had very serious drawbacks, however. It required you to divide the little time you have in town between the conference and the local friends with whom you're staying. Friends expect you to do much socializing with them, such as having breakfasts, lunches, and dinners with them, plus a little sightseeing, along with those long kitchen-table sessions at the end of the day talking about old times. Regrettably religious conferences had their own rigid schedules and social agendas that had to be respected, she reminded herself.

Therefore she was pleased when she was able to get her plane ticket much cheaper than budgeted. Now she could stay at the hotel with the other delegates, which would allow her to renew old acquaintances, as well as network with other preachers and ministerial people from around the country. And, of course, there would be those lively get-togethers at the end of the official day that she always looked forward to. Some of the best gospel singers and musicians in the country attended those conferences. Usually after a long day of conference activities, in the nearby all-night coffee shops there would be musical dueling among the various singing groups, with white folks thinking they were crazy. This was always lots of fun. She usually joined in the singing and the merriment.

After the conference she planned to take a couple of days and go to Georgia to do some research on their family tree.

Rev. Flowers sat at her desk in the quiet of her office and thanked the Lord for giving her a few minutes of peace and comfort. Before her lay two Bibles: her father's Bible that she had always assumed was the family Bible, and the old Bible that Aunt Belle said was the real family Bible. The family history pages in her father's Bible began and ended with the "Crombies," their family name, with plenty of information on the Crombie family, including birthdays, dates of death, and notes on the family.

The other Bible, despite all the cross outs and eraser marks, clearly belonged to a family named "Busterson." In that Bible the pages that should have contained the family information had been ripped out, and there was no mention of the Crombies anywhere. Trying to make sense of things, Rev. Flowers had carefully gone through that Bible several times, page by page, looking for notations and other scribbles that would shed some light on who the Bustersons were, but she found nothing.

She even made a few long-distance telephone calls to older relatives around the country to see if they could help with this mystery. The calls were to relatives on her mother's side of the family, since everyone on her father's side of the family was now dead. The calls were of little help. No one on that side of the family had heard of the Bustersons. As her Aunt Jennie said to her on the telephone, "If that Bible contains a family secret of some kind, then Aunt Belle took it to the grave with her."

Rev. Flowers hadn't realized until now how little she and Lettie really knew about their paternal side of the family. As with most families, the information on her maternal and paternal sides of the family was very lopsided, for her mother's side of the family had done a much better job with their family tree and family history. A much better job of passing genealogical information down to their offsprings. In fact, that side of the family was very serious about their genealogy.

For example, she and Lettie knew that their great, great grandfather Horace Jennings on their mother's side went to Sacramento in the Great California Gold Rush in the 1840s and struck one of the richest gold mines in the Sacramento area. Grandpa Jennings was a very sensible man who neither smoked, drank, nor gambled. Sacramento was then a bustling frontier town that had sprung up overnight due to the influx of fortune hunters from around the world seeking gold, with its share of gamblers and whores.

When Grandpa Jennings' gold mine petered out, instead of throwing his money away chasing more gold, he packed up his winnings and went to Wyoming, where he settled down, married, and raised a family. Some family members maintained that he became an even richer man in Wyoming from all his various business enterprises there.

The family knew how Grandpa Jennings got to Wyoming. While gold mining in California, he befriended some people from Wyoming who told him about all the good things about Wyoming, so he moved there as the place where he wanted to settle down and invest the money he made in California. The big challenge in the family's genealogical search in Wyoming was determining how he met their great, great grandmother. For a long time this was a big mystery. Who was Grandmother Jennings? How did her family get to Wyoming, a state with so few black people? The few blacks in the state in those days were mostly cowboys, many married to Indian women. Was Grandma Jennings' family cowboys? Was she Indian? Was she a white woman? Where did she come from? How did she and Grandpa Jennings meet?

For years those questions remained unanswered; then one day the family found a listing for Grandma Jennings in the 1880 census records that revealed she was Negro. Other than that, they could find nothing else on her.

Then one of Viola's aunts went to Wyoming and visited the cemetery where Grandpa Jennings and Grandma Jennings were buried, but the modest headstones revealed nothing. The aunt returned home empty-handed. One day another relative serendipitously came across something on the internet that appeared promising. It was a website of a white family in Cheyenne, Wyoming that alluded to a female foster child in their family in the mid 1800s who was "Negro." It said the five-year-old child was born in Oklahoma. With that new information Viola's family pursued their genealogical research on Grandma Jennings with increased vigor.

Their renewed search resulted in another aunt returning to Wyoming to visit the graveyard of the white family on the internet that had the black child. In Wyoming she found an inscription on the headstone of one of the white matriarchs that read: "She went to her grave eternally thankful to God for sending her that adorable little black angel who became the joy of her life."

The search next led to long hours in the Cheyenne library reading old newspapers from the period. Then as Grandpa Jennings had done more than a hundred years earlier, this aunt struck gold. She found a newspaper article telling how in 1835 a white family took in a little Negro girl who was the sole survivor of an Indian attack on a wagon train of Negroes moving to the Northwest. The newspaper story surmised that the trail where the black bodies were found had been a seldom-used trail since it hadn't been ground into dust like the more traveled routes used by the white wagon trains. The Negroes had brought livestock with them because carcasses of milk cows were found in the carnage. The article also speculated that the black settlers were escaped slaves migrating west.

"Her parents were pioneers killed in an Indian raid, and some white people found her and raised her," Viola's aunt said when calling home excited about what she had learned about Grandma Jennings. The family was satisfied that all the bits of information matched, and that they had discovered their great, great grandmother's Wyoming origin.

Viola wished she could go back that far on her father's side of the family. There seemed to be a big black hole on that side of the family. It was so frustrating. She wished she had talked more with Aunt Belle about it when she was alive. She deeply regretted not being able to find the time to visit Aunt Belle in the nursing home before she died. But her church was going through rocky financial times that year that required all of her time and energy. That summer Aunt Belle died peacefully in her sleep in a nursing home in Georgia, and it was Aunt Jennie who notified them of Aunt Belle's death.

Because Aunt Jennie had been so close to Aunt Belle over the years and lived near her in Georgia, Rev. Flowers asked her to handle Aunt Belle's meager estate. The house, land and small bank account were used to clear up Aunt Belle's nursing home and medical bills, and the one insurance policy she had was barely large enough to bury her. Viola and Lettie let Aunt Jennie keep what she wanted from Aunt Belle's things and dispose of everything else that had no value.

Viola and Lettie learned that before her death Aunt Belle gave Aunt Jennie the family Bible, or what she said was the family Bible, to give to Viola, the oldest sister. Like their other maternal relatives, Aunt Jennie knew nothing about the Busterson family and told Viola that she never heard Aunt Belle ever mention that name. "Aunt Belle never talked much about her family in Georgia. She always changed the subject like it pained her to talk about it. The only family she talked about were you guys," Aunt Jennie said, adding that she often wondered why Aunt Belle was so reticent about her family. She recalled in particular how sullen Aunt Belle would become whenever asked why her family moved up North.

Chapter Fifteen

Later that night after she finished packing for her trip to St. Louis, Rev. Flowers went into her study and sat down. She couldn't stop thinking about the Bustersons. It was Aunt Jennie who got her thinking that perhaps her paternal family changed their names after moving up North. Viola knew that many immigrant families in Cherry Bluffs changed their names when they came to America. Cherry Bluffs was the town in Iowa where Viola and Lettie were raised as children. Her childhood friend Irene Radnik told her once that when her parents first came to this country from Czechoslovakia, their family name was "Zahradnick," which they shortened to just "Radnik" because people in this country had so much trouble pronouncing and spelling their real name.

"Daddy's first name is really Cermak, but the men at the plant kept calling him Mac. So to his friends at work, he became just Mac Radnik," little Irene told little Viola that day.

"You mean he changed his name just like that," the black child asked, amazed.

"A lot of Czech people changed their names. Our next-door neighbors, the Jeds, are really the 'Jedlickas,' and the Proctors down the street are really the 'Prochazkas.' My mother's real name is 'Apolenka,' not 'Lena,' " the white girl giggled, thinking it was funny.

"What's your real name then?" Vi asked, now confused.

"You know my real name. Irene Radnick. It's even on my birth certificate."

The little girls returned to playing house.

Now an adult, Rev. Flowers sat there alone wondering if her father and grandfather had changed their family name like the Radnicks had done. She knew that black people sometimes changed their names as well. She remembered the Fosters, an African American family who lived across the street from them in Iowa and attended her father's church when she was a child. Mr. Foster coached the local amateur team of Czech and black boxers at the neighborhood youth center that won several Golden Gloves regional championships.

She recalled vividly that Saturday afternoon when a string of squad cars sped onto their block and stopped in front of the Fosters, where Mr. Foster was entertaining friends at a barbecue in his backyard. The policemen got out of their cars with guns drawn, causing all the neighbors to come out into their yards to see what was going on. Some of the policemen went to the front door, while others went around to the backyard where all the festivities were. A few minutes later they returned to their cars with Mr. Foster in handcuffs.

Viola learned later that Mr. Foster was really a man named Frank Steel who had escaped from prison in Indiana and had settled down and become a model citizen in Cherry Bluffs. In fact he was her Sunday school teacher for years. She recalled that shortly after Mr. Foster's arrest, the Foster family moved away. She and Susie Foster were in grammar school together.

Could that be what happened in her family? She remembered the story about her Uncle Rufus, her grandfather's younger brother who, according to family lore, was always getting into trouble with the law. "Whatever happened to him?" she wondered aloud. When growing up she seldom heard his name mentioned around the house, and even Aunt Belle never talked about him. Viola just assumed that Uncle Rufus died before she and Lettie were born. She asked Aunt Belle about him a few times, but Aunt Belle just made a face and muttered that little grunting sound she always made when annoyed with something. Then she would change the subject.

Uncle Rufus was a mystery if there ever was one. There was a story that he was chased out of the South because he messed around with a white woman. Was that story true? Was that why Viola's grandfather suddenly left the South and possibly changed the family name from Busterson to Crombie?

Upon thinking about it more, the story about Uncle Rufus didn't make any sense, Rev. Flowers concluded, because in the old days when young black men got into serious trouble with the law, they usually fled the area alone, not with their entire family. In the dark of night the young man would bundle up a few things, kiss his weeping mother good-bye, look at his disappointed father sheepishly, maybe shake his hand, and then head out into the night alone to hop the first freight train going North. By morning when the white authorities came looking for him, he would be long gone. As a rule, black families don't obliterate their entire family history just because one member of the family gets into trouble with the law. Black men are always getting into trouble with the law. The offending family member owes it to the family to leave home so as to keep the family safe.

The rumor about Uncle Rufus had it that the white girl's father was the leader of the local Ku Klux Klan. Maybe that was why the entire family fled, inasmuch as Klansmen back in those days were notorious for arriving on horseback, hooded in white sheets, with burning torches, tormenting black people on their hate list. Sometimes they were there to lynch a particular person, or sometimes to burn the whole family out. In either case, the Klan just being there struck fear in the hearts of black people near and far. That was the purpose of the Klan: to keep Negroes in their place by invoking fear.

"Did Uncle Rufus leave a family of his own?" Rev. Flowers asked herself, "A family somewhere that we don't know about. That might be something Lettie should look into in her research." Now she wished she had handled Aunt Belle's estate herself; those old papers and things might have held some answers, she thought.

"O Blessed Jesus!" she moaned at the all the anguish that old Bible was causing.

Chapter Sixteen

Viola Flowers, nee Crombie, was born in Iowa, but her family was originally from Georgia. Their family history had it that when their grandfather was a young man his entire family moved up North under very suspicious circumstances. When older on trips to Georgia to visit her Aunt Belle, Viola heard many different stories about why her family left the South.

One story had it that her grandfather's young brother Rufus got into such serious trouble with the law that it placed the entire family in jeopardy. Consequently, one morning before dawn her grandfather packed everyone into a horse-drawn wagon, including his widowed mother, and vanished from Georgia. The family then consisted of her grandfather, then a young bachelor, his widowed mother, his younger brother Rufus, and his sister Belle (Aunt Belle). Being the oldest son, her grandfather was the man of the house.

The two Crombie brothers were a study in contrast. Viola's grandfather was a stern, hardworking, religious man, whereas his young brother Rufus was a good-for-nothing roustabout who was always getting into scrapes with the law. According to the story, one year at age fifteen, just before cotton-picking time, Rufus ran off to a big city up North, where he stayed without ever contacting the family until he returned home a few years later to hide from some toughs looking for him. As the story went, upon returning home to the South, Rufus became romantically involved with Claire Stinson, who was not only white but was the only daughter of Ben Stinson, the leader of the local Ku Klux Klan. One morning Claire Mae's body was found in the woods. She had put a revolver in her mouth and pulled the trigger. Days later the noise of wild dogs fighting over her remains attracted the attention of passing hunters. The medical examiner reported that at the time of her death she was four months pregnant with a black baby.

On hearing the news of Claire Stinson's pregnancy, everybody in the black section of town knew Rufus was the father, for he had openly boasted about Claire Stinson to his black friends. Some say that he even took her dancing a few times at Moody's Place, a black juke joint well known for its bootleg liquor.

Ben Stinson swore on his mother's grave that when he discovered who the father was, he would tar and feather the nigger. According to the story, when learning of Ben Stinson's threat, Viola's grandfather that night hurriedly packed the entire family into a wagon, including his younger brother Rufus, and fled North. He knew that the Klan when sufficiently enraged often wiped out entire Negro families. Other than the part about the sheriff's daughter killing herself, there was no proof that anything else in the story had happened. Everything else was mere speculation or hearsay, including the part about the pregnancy.

Another story had it that one week in the early 1900s it rained so heavily in the small rural Georgia county where Viola's grandfather lived that the river began to overflow its banks. This was during the depths of an economic depression when unemployment was so high and farm prices so low that it didn't pay to pick the cotton in the fields. Economic times were so bad that even the large property owners had trouble keeping their plantations out of foreclosure. The townspeople—mostly poor white farmers and lowly black sharecroppers—could barely raise enough food on their acreages to keep their families from starving. Barnyard animals had to be slaughtered and eaten, and the nearby woods were nearly hunted out because of all the hungry people seeking wild game to put food on their tables at night.

Consequently, instead of heeding the urgent call to report to the river banks to help hold back the raging waters, the townspeople began packing their things and leaving. White and black families alike. To them staying there simply wasn't worth fighting the angry river for. Hence what started as a mere trickle quickly turned into a torrent of frightened people fleeing the county in horse-drawn wagons and old cars and trucks, leaving their homes to the ravages of the flood. The story was that Viola's grandfather worked half a morning helping with the levee, then he too hurried home, harnessed up his horses, packed his family into a wagon, and left with the others, except he left the South entirely.

Once Viola asked her Aunt Belle (her grandfather's sister) about all those conflicting stories. "Why did Grandpa really leave the South, Aunt Belle?" she asked.

"What does your Poppa say?" Aunt Belle replied guardedly.

"Daddy says you guys moved to Missouri because a church there offered Grandpa a better job. He said Grandpa's old ministry was only part-time, and the scrimpy collections on Sunday barely paid Grandpa's horse feed bills."

Aunt Belle didn't comment one way or another.

Whatever the reason, their family moved from Georgia to Missouri where Viola's grandfather started all over again in St. Louis with great success. The first day in town he lucked upon a small black gospel church that had just lost its pastor. In fact it was the pastor's funeral at the church that caught his attention that day as he walked past the crowd of mourners outside the church. Because there weren't enough men at the funeral, the pallbearers were having trouble getting the coffin out the church door so it could be taken to the colored cemetery. Viola's grandfather, a stranger in town, stepped out of the crowd of onlookers and helped the men lift the heavy body of their pastor into the hearse. Viola's grandfather ended up going to the cemetery with the mourners, where he took over the burial ceremony and delivered the rites before the body was lowered into the ground.

The mourners from the church left the cemetery with a brand new pastor: the Reverend T. J. Crombie, Viola's beloved grandfather. They must have thought that this big, good-looking stranger had been sent to them by God. Not only did he become their pastor, he became one of the most powerful black clergymen in the Midwest. Under his leadership, that little gospel church grew into one of the mightiest black churches in St. Louis, where eventually he became bishop. The church got even larger after he broke away from the mother church. This was long before Viola and Lettie were born.

The story of how her family got from Missouri to Iowa was much clearer. One summer Viola's father, then a young ordained minister, was sent by his father up to Iowa to start a branch church there. That same year Aunt Belle went back to Georgia to live, the only family member to return to the South. While Viola's grandfather had to struggle financially for years to get his church going in St. Louis, the young Rev. Tom Crombie, Jr., her father, had a rather easy time getting his new branch church off the ground. Although there weren't many Negroes living in Iowa at the time, Rev. Thomas J. Crombie, Sr. had traveled and preached in that state for years, often taking his young son Tom with him. Black churches there invited him back year after year. In Cherry Bluffs, Iowa, some townsfolk encouraged him to set up a Church of God & Spirit in their town. Thus when young Tom Jr. was ordained, his father sent him to Cherry Bluffs to establish a branch church there. By then blacks had begun moving into town in larger numbers to work in the meat packing plant that needed their menial labor.

Rev. Thomas J. Crombie, Jr. met Viola's mother in Iowa where they fell in love, married, and had Viola and Lettie, with Viola being the firstborn. Viola's mother's family was from Georgia as well.

For a black family in a town where most black people worked as common laborers in dirty factory jobs, life was fairly comfortable for them in Iowa. When the church was getting started in Iowa, most of young Rev. Tom Crombie's salary, as well as the money he needed to buy their first home, came from the mother church in St. Louis, then one of the largest and wealthiest black churches in that part of the country. The St. Louis church was the home office of the Church of Christ & Spirit, the national church that now had affiliate churches around the nation.

When a small girl growing up in Iowa, Viola's two best friends were Betty Harris and Irene Radnik. Betty Harris was a black girl Viola's age who lived in the nearby small town of Lyonshead, Iowa, where their family was the only black family in town. Irene Radnik was a white girl Viola's age who lived just around the corner from Viola. Irene Radnik went to a Catholic school, whereas Viola attended a public school. Viola and Irene played together every day after school. Viola and Betty Harris played together mostly on Sundays when the latter's family, because there were no black churches in Lyonshead, came to Cherry Bluffs for church services.

Sometimes when there was nothing going on at the church, Viola and Irene would play in the back pews where they would play house with their dolls. Rev. Tom Crombie, Jr., a kind and considerate man, didn't mind, provided they kept the noise down so he could work in his little office in the back. He liked seeing children play on the front steps of the church or in the church itself, because it showed God at work playing with the little children, he would say.

At first Irene Radnik found it hard to believe that there wasn't more to Violet's church, since it seemed so small in comparison to her own large, elaborately adorned Catholic church over on Third Avenue. To Irene, Viola's church was more like the little one-room school house she had attended before her family left the farm and moved into Cherry Bluffs so her father could get a job at the Iron Works.

"Where's your confession booth?" little Irene asked Viola the first time she saw the inside of the small Negro gospel church. The little white girl looked around and wondered where everything was. So much was missing.

"A what?"

"You know, the place where you go and tell the priest about your sins."

With her doll in her arms, the little black girl pointed to the moaners' bench down front by the pulpit. "If you're a sinner and want to come forward and repent and join the church, you do it right there."

The sinner's bench was where little Viola went when she was "saved." She was only six at the time, an age her mother thought was a little too young for a child to become a Christian.

"Tom, is Viola old enough to take responsibility for her sins?" her mother queried Viola's father at the time.

"Of course she is. Viola's one of God's miracles. She was born understanding the words of God," he answered proudly.

Little Viola had asked to join the church after she had overheard her father planning for the children scheduled to be "saved" on the first night of the big church revival that week. "I'm ready too, Daddy. I'm ready to accept Christ," she stepped up and said eagerly.

Viola Flowers remembered the day when she was saved like it was only yesterday. She even recalled the name of the visiting evangelist who preached that night, remembering even what he looked like. He was big, fat, and sweaty with bad breath. With his white silk handkerchief waving in the air as he preached, he smelled of stale tobacco, despite that their church didn't allow smoking.

In the middle of his sermon, the big black bear leaped from the pulpit and loomed over the children with his huge chest out and large paws waving high in the air. At the top of his lungs he screamed out for their souls. Her soul. It frightened Viola to death. A teenager on the bench next to her fainted from fright. That night after she was saved, little Viola cried copious tears of joy, for she believed that now Jesus would always be there with her, holding her hand, giving her lots of hugs and kisses. It was the most exciting night of her young life.

Most kids Viola knew didn't get "saved" until they were much older. Most of them dreaded that day of reckoning, particularly the boys who realized they would have to give up all their bad habits, such as throwing stones at stray dogs, having pissing and spitting contests, and playing marbles for keeps, which was seen as gambling by their church.

While her little white Catholic friend looked on in disbelief, Viola pointed to the pews in her small church. "If you just want to testify, you can do it anywhere. You just get up from your seat and tell Jesus that you're sorry for your sins."

Though she didn't tell Irene this, just last night during church services, on the very spot where Irene was standing, an old woman broke into tears and got to her feet and begged God to forgive her for lying about another church member. Another old woman sitting next to her got up and started repenting also. She was followed by two more old ladies. "Forgive us, dear Jesus! Please forgive us! We meant no harm! We shouldn't have listened to the Devil!" they chorused in agony to the reproving "Amens" around them.

All of the congregation, including Rev. Tom, knew that the four old women had spread a false rumor about a young girl's being pregnant. Because of all the shame, the girl ran away from home and now couldn't be found. The girl, her grieving parents, and the four old ladies were all members of Rev. Tom's church. What the old women did had greatly distressed the entire church, but after they testified and prayed, all was forgiven.

Little Viola told Irene, "Or if the spirit hits you, you just get up during the service and tell everybody what's you're feeling. Tell them how much you love Jesus, and what he means in your life. Sometimes you're so filled with joy that you want to dance and thank Jesus for your just being alive. Thank him for standing by you and loving you."

Little Viola always turned warm and glowing when discussing her beloved Jesus. She pointed to where all the brothers and sisters of the church were dancing last night. She even pointed to the church windows because sometimes when the service was very lively and the church was packed to the rafters, onlookers from outside, though not members, would join in the rejoicing. Sometimes they would testify and praise the Lord from out-of-doors. If the minister saw them out there, he would wave for them to come in and join the other sinners repenting down front. Sometimes he went out and dragged them by the arm into the church.

The little white Catholic girl just stood there dumbfounded by this strange religion.

"Where does the priest sleep? Back there?" the white girl pointed naively to the small backroom where Rev. Tom Crombie had his cubby-hole of an office next to the broom closet. In those days most black churches, particularly gospel churches, were very modest structures.

"We Christians don't have priests. We have ministers of God," Viola answered sharply as if annoyed by Irene's ignorance.

"We're Christians too."

"No, you're not. You're Catholic, and Catholics aren't Christian."

"We are too," the white girl countered, nearly in tears.

"Maybe you are, but Elder Davis says you're not," Viola said, backing off some after realizing she was being a bit mean.

The two little girls went back to playing house.

Usually on Fridays Irene spent more time at Viola's house than the other days of the week. Viola didn't mind, except it complicated things when the Harris family sometimes brought Betty over on Fridays to spend the weekend at Viola's. Due to their jealousy over Viola, Irene Radnik and Betty Harris didn't like each other. When the three girls were together, Irene and Betty fought constantly. Even though she was white and Betty black, Irene saw Betty as an interloper.

"Why don't you stay in Lyonshead where you belong," Irene would fuss at Betty when angry at her about something, a very ironic remark since the Town of Lyonshead was all-white except for the Harrises.

Viola saw reconciling the quarreling girls as one of her Christian duties. "You two shouldn't be fighting like that. We're all God's children," she would tell them sounding like an adult. This would work for a while until the little blue-eyed Irene and the little brown-eyed Betty would resume scratching and clawing each other like two angry cats.

Fridays were notable for another reason. Frequently Irene came over to Viola's house early on Fridays to escape the awful tension in her home on Friday afternoons. Almost every week at around the same time of day, Irene's home would begin to fill with dread. Every Friday just after lunch, Irene's mother, a stay-at-home housewife (in those days few women worked outside the home), would start pacing the floor worried about how much money her husband would bring home after cashing his weekly paycheck at Leo's. Leo's was a gin mill near the plant where most of the factory men stopped and cashed their paychecks on Friday afternoons. Irene's father worked as a common laborer at the Acme Iron Works where he hired on after failing at farming.

Check-cashing at Leo's was free, but Leo Stancek expected the men who worked in the plants nearby to at least buy a few drinks in his place. On paydays the responsible men who cashed their checks at Leo's would have a beer or two, eat a few pickled sausages from the big jars on the bar, and have a few laughs with the boys. Then they would take the balance of their weekly salary home to their wives.

Unfortunately, though, there were men like Irene's dad who would cash their checks and start drinking at Leo's and wouldn't stop until all their money was gone. Then they would stagger home drunk, broke, and pissed off at their own stupidity. Often if their wives asked about their paychecks, the wives got beatings. It was awful. Irene's drunken father regularly slapped her mother around on Friday nights, giving her fat lips and black eyes. He was a nice man when sober. This was behavior characteristic of many factory workers in that part of town, whether Czech, Irish, Syrian, black or Native American.

"Once Mama had to be taken to the hospital," Irene told Viola one day, her small round face void of emotion. Her remark was so matter-of-fact that she could have been talking about one of her mother's recipes that the two girls often shared when playing with their toy kitchen sets.

"Why don't your mama do like Mrs. Enderson does?" Viola suggested. The men's pissing away their weekly paychecks on Fridays was a serious problem in their workingclass neighborhood. This was a topic Viola had heard her father discuss many times with church elders. (Those were the old days before automatic payroll bank deposits.) He had even given sermons on the topic.

Viola was referring to the Enderson family. The Enderson father was a slightly built black man with only one eye and a crippled left leg whom the guys at the plant fondly called "Sparky." He worked as a butcher on the Hog Kill at Ward's Packinghouse. He was one of the hardest working employees at the plant. He was certainly the fastest. With him on the assembly line, the hog kill department would regularly finish an eight-hour kill of hogs in less than five hours. When they did so, under union rules they could go home three hours early while still being paid for eight hours.

On paydays on Fridays, the men worked even faster. In his sleeveless shirt, his face dripping sweat, his knife flashing red with blood as hogs sped through the line hanging on large hooks, Sparky would exhort his coworkers at the top of his lungs to speed it up and empty the hog pens so they all could go home early. Most of the animals arrived by rail from Omaha on a daily basis.

Around midmorning Sparky would begin shouting like a college cheer leader, "Let's go! Let's go! Let's get out of here. Daisy's waiting at Leo's!" The production line would begin moving like an express train that had just upped its speed gauge. In their hurry to get home early on Fridays to start their weekend, the hog kill gang wouldn't stop for lunch and would slaughtered their eight-hour allotment of animals in only four hours, sometimes in even less time. And then they were out the front gate of the plant like a herd of wild horses, on their way to Leo's Tavern. On the beef kill side of the plant, the workers were moving through the cattle just as fast.

Daisy was the pretty Czech barmaid at Leo's who would be waiting for them and their paychecks. At Leo's, Sparky Enderson would drink beer after beer until his check was all gone or until he passed out, whichever occurred first. A real goodtime Charley, for as long as his money lasted, he would generously buy everybody drinks, and for years week after week he would stagger home drunk and broke. It was so bad that his family was often forced to go to the church for welfare aid to survive the week. It was extra painful for the Enderson children who frequently had to go without food until assistance could be found. What made it so tragic was that Sparky Enderson was an excellent worker who hadn't missed a day's work in over twenty years.

Then thank God, Rev. Tom's church got involved. One afternoon a few days before payday, Rev. Tom and Mrs. Enderson went to Leo's and worked out a deal with Leo Stancek wherein Leo would cash Sparky's check every week and then give him a few dollars so he could have his night out, including enough to play the jukebox which Sparky loved to do when he got drunk and became melancholy. Leo would then keep the rest of the money in an envelope in the cash register until Mrs. Enderson came for it the next day.

The arrangement with Leo worked out quite well. Sparky had his Friday nights out, and his family got most of his paycheck. The church called it the "Enderson Plan," and other wives began using it.

"Do you want me to ask my father to take your mother and work out something with Mr. Stancek at Leo's?" Viola asked, now sounding like a social worker.

"Would your father do that for us? We're Catholic?" the white girl asked with wide unbelieving eyes.

"That's O.K. Mr. Stancek's Catholic, too," Viola said as the girls went back to their play.

Viola first met Betty Harris when Betty's parents started bringing their whole family over from Lyonshead, Iowa, to Rev. Tom's church in Cherry Bluffs, Iowa. Because there were no black churches in Lyonshead, the Harris family made the twenty-mile trip to Cherry Bluffs nearly every Sunday. As the big cities of Des Moines and Omaha were always exciting for little Viola to visit because of all the black people living there, coming to Cherry Bluffs on weekends from the small town of Lyonshead was just as exciting for little Betty Harris. Accustomed to seeing only white faces in Lyonshead, she was fascinated by all the black people, or what she thought were a lot of black people, in Cherry Bluffs.

Sometimes when Betty's family brought Betty over to Cherry Bluffs on Friday evenings so she could spend the weekend with Viola before church on Sunday, Betty's parents would stay with old friends across town, and go out with them on Saturday nights since there were no black places of entertainment in Lyonshead.

While Viola was a serious, religious child, Betty was a carefree, fun-loving little girl who had an eye for the boys even at that young age. Other than her big brother, there were no black boys in Lyonshead.

"I'm going to be a singer when I grow up, and move to Chicago," Betty would often say to Viola when they played together. Betty's aunt was a singer who lived in Chicago and sang in a jazz band there.

Betty thought her aunt was the most glamorous woman on earth, and she wanted to be exactly like her when she grew up. Viola first met Betty's aunt when the aunt attended church with the Harrises on one of her visits from Chicago. Because Betty's aunt brought Viola a nice gift and took her and Betty out for ice-cream sundaes after church that day, Viola liked her. Rev. Tom also liked Betty's aunt, for whenever she came to church he knew he would find a crisp twenty dollar bill in the offing plate, an extraordinary sum for his small church in those days.

Some of the church sisters, however, didn't like Betty's aunt whom they saw as being too much "of the world" due to her short tight skirts, bright high-heeled shoes, and hip-wiggling walk. Some speculated viciously that she was a prostitute in Chicago, not a singer as the Harrises had said.

When the girls were about seven or eight years old, on one of Betty Harris' overnight visits, Viola tried to talk Betty into joining the church. At first Betty wanted nothing to do with being "saved." Although her parents were members of Rev. Tom's church, Betty feared that if she became saved she would have to give up many of the things she enjoyed in life that the church considered bad. Like lipstick and fingernail polish, for instance. Most of all, Betty feared that if she went down front and sat on the moaners' bench, she would become "possessed" and make a fool of herself by shouting and jumping up and down like she had seen others do when feeling the holy ghost. It was always very embarrassing. Once an old man's pants fell down after he jumped up and screamed and reached skyward for God.

Viola finally talked Betty Harris into agreeing to join the church, convincing her that the only way they could go to heaven together was for both of them to be saved. Because Viola was already saved, Betty agreed to be saved also.

"I'm bringing in a sinner tomorrow, Mama. A real big one," little Viola told her mother proudly.

"That's nice. Who is it?"

"Betty. She says she's ready to accept Christ."

"That's a big decision for someone her age. Did you speak to her parents about it?"

"No. She just decided a few minutes ago," Viola said, casting an eye at her bedroom where she had left Betty playing. "I told her there was nothing to be afraid of. That it was a lot like learning to swim. You just close your eyes and dive in."

"Shame on you, Viola! You shouldn't have told her that. It isn't like learning to swim. Betty must be ready to accept the word of the Lord. As I said, it's a big decision for a little girl to make all by herself."

"I'm a little girl and I made the decision all by myself a long time ago," little Viola replied.

"Yes, you did. But remember, honey, you discussed it with me and your father first. Have Betty discuss it with her parents first, and if they approve, then maybe she can do it the next time she comes over," Mrs. Crombie said, patting Viola on the head for trying to save the soul of her good friend.

"That girl's gonna make a good evangelist someday," she chuckled to her husband later.

But Betty Harris never joined the church; the Harris family moved to St. Louis when Betty was still in high school, from where she and Viola continued their close friendship. In fact, it was her friendship with Betty that helped Viola get through her stormy romance with Rev. Manny Scott.

Chapter Seventeen

While Rev. Viola Flowers had her father's gentle heart and easy disposition, she had her grandfather's toughness, his fierce determination, and his strong leadership ability. This was a rare combination for one person. Most of all, she had her grandfather's ability to take forceful action when needed. A good example of her grandfather's legendary forcefulness was how as pastor of his Missouri church in his younger days he handled the pregnancies of young unmarried members of his church. This was before he became bishop of the national church. It was said that when an unmarried girl in his church became pregnant, he wouldn't rest until he discovered the identity of the young man responsible, and he wouldn't stop until he made that young man marry the girl.

"You ruined this poor girl's virtue because you couldn't control your lust. Well, now you must pay for it. You must take full responsibility for what you've done. You must marry this girl and give the baby a name and a home," he would wag his finger at the father of the unborn child. No young man in town wanted to be so confronted by Rev. T.J. Crombie. They knew he had a closet full of shotguns. When learning they had gotten a member of Rev. Crombie's church pregnant, most young men, out of fear of Rev. Crombie, would step forward immediately and marry the girl voluntarily. Other young men would get out of town as fast as possible, some hopping freight trains going north.

Usually those pregnancies resulted from one-night stands or from high school friends just messing around and going too far. Often the men were older males taking advantage of gullible teenage girls.

Although most of the young men that Rev. Crombie marched to the altar by the ear were black, there were a few white guys in the group as well. For instance, when Ernestine Green's parents learned that Ernestine was pregnant, they called in Rev. Crombie who quizzed the teenage girl about who the father was. Ernestine finally broke down and tearfully confessed that Ralph Armstrong, a white boy, was the father of the baby ballooning in her stomach.

Ralph Armstrong was the youngest son of Earl Armstrong who ran the hardware store a few blocks from where the Greens lived. It seemed that one day when Ernestine walked by the hardware store, young Ralph Armstrong winked at her. This led to her flirting with him in return, which eventually led to their meeting nights at the hardware store after the store closed, where they made love on a cot in the backroom. And she became pregnant. When she became so large that she couldn't keep her condition to herself any longer, she told her parents that she was pregnant, but refused to name the boy. Her parents, longtime members of the Church of God & Spirit, took the matter to Rev. Crombie, who got her to talk.

"Ralphie says he loves me," Ernestine sobbed when revealing the boy's identity to Rev. Crombie and her parents.

Rev. Crombie told her parents that he would speak to the parents of the white boy. "Leave this to me. The Lord and I will take care of this," he told the girl's parents when they wanted to come with him. He advised them that it would be best if he handled the matter with only himself and their daughter. They were in Missouri, a state with its share of Negro lynchings. Rev. Crombie knew that a clerical collar was the only thing a black person had that came close to serving as a badge in white neighborhoods.

He dragged Ernestine by the arm to the white shopkeeper's home. When he knocked on the front door, the white family was having dinner. Young Ralph saw Ernestine and knew immediately why she was there. He looked around the table shamefacedly and then tried to hide behind his mashed potatoes.

"Good evening, folks. Sorry to disturb your dinner. I'm Rev. Crombie from the Church of God & Spirit over on Sixth Street. This is Ernestine Green, a member of my church. May we have a word with you outside?" Rev. Crombie said to the stern-faced white man sitting at the head of the dinner table, craning as he spoke past the small freckled-faced boy who had answered the door.

Wondering what the Negroes wanted, the burly white man swiped his mouth, put his napkin down, and got up from the table. He went outside and joined the black minister and the girl. Then the three of them moved farther out into the yard so they could talk without being heard from inside the house.

"This is Ernestine Green, a member of my church. She has something she wants to tell you," Rev. Crombie introduced the girl again.

"Hi Mr. Armstrong. I'm Ernestine Green. My father shops at your store. I come in with him sometimes to buy nails and things." She hesitated for a second or so, looked apprehensively at Rev. Crombie, and then said dumbly sounding like a girl scout selling cookies, "I'm pregnant and Ralph's the father."

"My son, Ralph?" The white man's jaw dropped, his face turned blood red.

"Yessir. Didn't Ralphie tell you? He said he was gonna to tell you and Mrs. Armstrong so we can get married."

Without a word the white man grabbed the black girl by the hand and pulled her back into the house. Rev. Crombie followed behind her protectively.

Ignoring the other family members, Mr. Armstrong marched the girl angrily before his 20-year-old son still eating at the table and asked him sharply, "Do you know this girl?"

"Yes Sir."

"She says she's pregnant with your child? Is that true?"

Young Ralph looked sheepishly at his mother, then his grandmother, and then at his brothers and sisters. The rest of the Armstrong family looked on in horror like a boatload of people suddenly beset by a horrible storm. At first Ralph wanted to deny he was the baby's father so as to make it a case of his word against hers, in which case he knew he would win. Then he looked at his scowling father, and at the no-nonsense face of the Negro minister.

"That's what she says," he parried the question nervously, still avoiding Ernestine's big brown eyes.

"And what do you say about it?" his father replied.

"We want the truth, Ralphie?" his mother pleaded, sounding like she was about to cry. The grandmother was already sobbing.

"It's probably mine," the young man confessed honestly, barely audible, his strict moral upbringing winning out. His eyes welled with tears over what he had done. He knew he had taken the pretty colored girl's virginity. After he and Ernestine had sex that first night, he told his best buddy, who then wanted him to find him a nice colored girlfriend whom he could screw. But Ralph was afraid to ask Ernestine about it, knowing her strict religious views and all.

He knew she wasn't even supposed to be dating. In fact, it surprised him when she let him kiss her the first time and didn't stop him when he started feeling her up. Their relationship lasted right up to the swelling up of the pregnancy.

Rev. Crombie stepped forward and took charge. "Mr. Armstrong, I need to know what you're going to do about this matter," he said in that big booming voice of his. He thought of Ernestine's parents at home waiting and worrying. He had to take them back some resolve.

"What're you talking about, Reverend?" Ralph's father said with a bemused look. With bulging eyes, he looked at his wife with fear when it dawned on him what the black minister might be talking about. Was it possible that the black girl was underage and that his son might have committed statutory rape?

"Earl, I think the Reverend's talking about what we're going to do about the baby," his wife said nervously.

While her husband was worried about the criminal law, Mrs. Armstrong was worried about what that poor girl was going to do about the baby. She had heard tales from her white friends about how cavalierly Negro women disposed of their unwanted babies. "Colored women get rid of unwanted babies like we throw food scraps into the garbage," one of her friends told her once.

Therefore Mrs. Armstrong, who normally opposed abortions, believed it was easy to get abortions in the Negro section of town, which in her mind might be a solution to their problem. This was untrue, of course: the truth was that because of economic, social, religious, and family reasons, it was twice as hard for black women than white women to get rid of unwanted pregnancies, which was why black women kept more of their illegitimate children than white women. This had always been the case down through American history.

"The Reverend's talking about abortion, Earl. The girl's going to need money to get rid of the baby," Mrs. Armstrong blurted out callously, in her distress forgetting about the children at the table. She looked at the black minister for concurrence.

"No-oooo!" the black girl threw up her arms and screamed, then broke into tears. To calm her down, Rev. Crombie took her in his arms and held her like a father would a daughter.

"Mrs. Armstrong, you should be ashamed of yourself. We're

sanctified people. We don't believe in abortions. Abortions are abominations in the eyes of the Lord. These young people must be married, and quickly," he bellowed at the white woman.

The Armstrongs sitting around the table dropped their knives and forks like there had just been an 8.2 earthquake. The grandmother's false teeth nearly fell out.

"You're talking about our little Ralphie marrying her?" the grandmother shrieked at the prospect of a Negro in their Scotch-Irish family. Ralphie's mother and sisters began to sob, while his father and brothers looked on stupidly.

"It's not what I want! It's what God demands!" Rev. Crombie's acerbic words bounced off the walls like the loud banging of a judge's gavel.

Two weeks later the couple was married in the Church of God & Spirit, with Rev. Crombie officiating. Both families, properly dressed for the occasion, were there in full attendance. Among others attending the wedding were the two other interracial families that had been brought together in a similar fashion.

Chapter Eighteen

In contrast to her grandfather, Rev. Flowers' father was a pliant man who because of his gentleness often gave the impression of being weak. But he wasn't a weak person. It took much courage to believe as he did in the New Testament teachings about "turning the other cheek." His philosophy was just the opposite of his famous father who believed in the Old Testament philosophy of "an eye for an eye, a tooth for a tooth." Like in most things involving her grandfather and father, Rev. Flowers came down somewhere in the middle. She even had a saying for it: "You love your enemy defensively."

While she had many of the kinder traits of her father, particularly his gentleness and his love of people, she had her grandfather's strength and political cunning. Her father was an unassuming man who more resembled a mild-mannered poet than a gospel preacher, and who didn't stand out much in a crowd. He ruled the national church by consensus and was masterful at getting people to agree on things. Contrast that with Viola Flowers' grandfather who dwarfed everything around him, and who in his day ruled the national church with an iron fist, brooking no insubordination.

Often Rev. Flowers' father's gentleness was interpreted as weakness by his enemies. Yes, enemies. Pastors have enemies. "In any Christian church, just being the pastor will create enemies for you. There'll always be a few members of the church who either won't like what you're saying in the pulpit or what you're doing in your pastoral duties. That's just the nature of our business," Viola's father told her once. Even in her father's time there were members of the Church of God & Spirit who wanted to break away on doctrinal grounds and start their own church. Splintering of the church was a constant threat.

During his rule her grandfather was very fortunate to always have strong lieutenants around him in the church. Powerful and loyal elders who helped him protect his throne. Some were so loyal that had he been a U.S. president they would've taken a bullet for him. Like with all despotic rulers, succession was his biggest worry. He hoped that his only son Tom Jr. would grow up to be strong enough—physically, mentally, morally, spiritually, theologically and politically—to take over the national church when he died. The national church was an affiliation of more than two hundred Church of God & Spirit churches around the country.

This was why he had been so hard on Tom Jr. when he was a boy. Back then he particularly disapproved of little Tom's daydreaming. As Aunt Belle told Viola once, "As a boy, your daddy used to get into trouble all the time for his daydreaming. When Tom caught Tom Jr. daydreaming, he used to slap him up side the head to bring him down to earth. Tom Jr.'s head was always up in the clouds. 'Daydreaming isn't praying, boy. Praying is giving your undivided attention to God, not dreaming about gallivanting through green fields chasing butterflies,' Tom Sr. used to scold him."

Tom Jr.'s gentleness disappointed his father deeply. Bishop Crombie in fact had such little confidence in Tom Jr. that when the latter graduated from the seminary and went to Iowa to set up an affiliate church there, Bishop Crombie sent Elder Simpson, one of his strongest church officers, along to look after his son. Elder Simpson even moved his family to Iowa when the new church was set up there.

Yet despite his easy disposition and low-keyed style, Rev. Tom Jr. had no serious palace revolts as leader of the Iowa church. Elder Simpson did a good job of surrounding the young minister with strong loyal elders selected largely from the people who had been the most active in seeking the Iowa church.

"As you all know, there are many people in this town who don't want this church to succeed. The Bishop's young son's gonna need your help in getting this church going. He's gonna need your loyalty and support. The Bishop's counting on you to stand by his son," Elder Simpson told the people of Iowa before agreeing to set up the branch church. Then he kept his eyes peeled for the people he thought would make good lieutenants for the young minister's army. And Elder Simpson made exceptional choices, for even after Elder Simpson died, members of the Iowa church stayed extremely loyal to the Bishop's gentle son.

Upon his father's death, Rev. Tom Jr.'s ascension to the Office of Presiding Bishop of the national church was also trouble free. Rev. Tom was amazed by how smoothly things went. Personally he believed that one of the older bishops should have gotten the position. Besides, he wasn't even a bishop himself at the time.

"Why me? You should be the new presiding bishop. You were Dad's right-hand man," Rev. Tom told Bishop Hazelton when Bishop Hazelton approached him upon his father's death about being the new head of the national church. Young Tom Jr. felt he didn't deserve the position.

Bishop Hazelton said something that was truly surprising to young Tom. "I've no interest in heading the church. Your father and I talked for years, even when you were a small boy, about you succeeding him when he died. This is something he always wanted. On his death bed he made me promise to support you for the position," the faithful second-in-command of the national church said. A large black man with thick shoulders, Bishop Hazelton looked more like an old, well-traveled heavyweight prizefighter than a preacher. But like Bishop Crombie, in the pulpit he had a voice that could set the world on fire.

"But you don't have to do this, Bishop Hazelton. Dad's dead, and the job should rightfully go to you. You've earned it. I'm fine where I am," Rev. Tom pleaded with the older man who had always been one of his heroes. He had always admired and respected the cagey old bishop who had stood by his father's side through thick and thin from the time the two of them left the Church of Christ many years ago as young men to start their own gospel church. All his life Rev. Tom had watched Bishop Hazelton strategize with his father at church meetings and conventions, and admired the working of his brilliant mind. He had watched him sweat and worry with his dad when things were rocky for the church. He had watched them pray together on matters of grave concern. Conversely, he had watched the two of them shout, sing, and clap hands together, even dance, at times of religious or family rejoicing. The old bishop was like a beloved uncle.

The old man's eyes took on the look of someone burdened with thoughts of his own mortality. "I'm your father's age, Reverend. I don't have much longer for this world. I don't have a son. Your father's dream that you take over the national church someday has always been my dream as well. I've watched you develop from the time you were a little boy. You've grown up to be a fine young man. You'll make a good national leader of the church. Please take the position and let this tired old man die in peace. I'm looking forward to joining your father. He and I have much work to do in heaven," the old gospel warrior said sadly. As he talked about how he and Bishop Crombie had worked together like brothers over the years, mist filled his puffy old eyes.

Rev. Tom was deeply touched by what Bishop Hazelton said. When alive his father never once talked to him about making him a bishop, let alone the presiding bishop of the national church. He had no idea that his father and Bishop Hazelton had that much confidence in him. Hence his astonishment.

Chapter Nineteen

Before accepting Bishop Hazelton's offer to become presiding bishop, like a seasoned negotiator, Viola's father set forth some conditions to Bishop Hazelton. "Before I accept being presiding bishop I must be assured that I'll have your full support in making the church more democratic. The church should belong to the people, not the clergy," he said.

The old bishop knew exactly what his friend's son was talking about. He realized that Bishop Crombie had ruled the national church with an iron hand. When Bishop Crombie established the national church he vested all church authority in two main bodies of the church: (1) the General Assembly and (2) the Executive Board which appointed the presiding bishop. In either case, like a dictator in any undemocratic state, the supreme power ended up in Bishop Crombie's hands.

Under the church's constitution, the General Assembly held the executive, legislative, and the judicial authority of the church. Bishop Crombie controlled the General Assembly through his power as the presiding bishop to appoint all the other bishops, pastors, elders, missionaries and lay members who made up the General Assembly. Between sessions of the General Assembly, the Executive Board held this power, subject to the veto power of the General Assembly. He controlled the Executive Board as well, because as presiding bishop he appointed the board members and served as board chairman. Some said Bishop Crombie had more power in his church than the Pope in Rome had in his.

"Don't be too hard on your father, Reverend. When we started the church we debated for months about how much voice the members should have in the affairs of the new church. Your father and I both believed in democracy deeply. But the main thing for both of us at the time was that, whatever the form of government of the church, our vision of the church had to be protected at all costs. We fought and worked too hard to have others come along later and change that vision. That was the big challenge. How do you protect the vision of something you love and cherish, while at the same time sharing it with others democratically? How do you share the power needed to make that vision a reality, without losing control of the vision itself? That's a devilish question, Reverend. The Catholic Church is still struggling with this problem. The infallibility of the Pope is being questioned by the Catholic laity more and more every day," he said.

He added pensively, "In setting up the church we really appreciated what the founding fathers of this country went through in setting up the country. They established an electoral college because they didn't fully trust the people. Assuring democracy for everybody is more that just a notion. It's the greatest challenge in human history. Achieving democracy is a much easier proposition than holding onto it once you get it. So your father and I agreed on a strong executive form of government. While we wanted more democracy, we didn't dare open the church up too much because of all the enemies lurking around waiting to steal the church back."

Rev. Tom offered his view, "To have real democracy we must fully trust the people. That's essential. It's my experience that the best decisions are the ones that come truly from the people. And I think our church is strong enough now to be run by the people."

"I hope you're right, Reverend. You do what you think is best and I'll back you," the old bishop said with resignation. "But remember, the political system we have in America today still only partially works. For us black folks it hardly works at all."

Rev. Tom accepted the position and became presiding bishop of the church.

Bishop Hazelton's confidence in his old friend's son was well placed. As new presiding bishop, Bishop Thomas Crombie, Jr. was a very popular leader of the national church. And he proved to be a real democrat. He immediately called for a Constitutional Convention that met and abolished the Office of the presiding bishop as set up by his father. The Constitution Convention then invested all church authority in a General Assembly elected by the various church memberships making up the national church. Under the new church constitution, the General Assembly was charged with choosing the Executive Board, which in turn was charged with making policy and rules, and conducting the affairs of the church when the General Assembly wasn't in session. All acts of the Executive Board, which served at the will of the General

Assembly, were subject to approval by the General Assembly. With the advice and consent of the General Assembly, the Executive Board appointed the various bishops, including the presiding bishop. Although appointed by the Executive Board, all the bishops served at the will of the General Assembly.

"I'll pray that you can keep it," Bishop Hazelton told the young presiding Bishop grimly when the constitutional changes were finally made, giving Rev. Tom Jr. his democracy.

Chapter Twenty

Some years before Bishop Tom Jr. took over as presiding bishop, Bishop Hazelton had brought in his nephew the Rev. C. P. Hazelton to run the church's fledgling publishing department. His nephew was an itinerant preacher and part-time printer. Because the publishing department was under Bishop Hazelton's jurisdiction, his nephew reported directly to him. Rev. C.P. Hazelton did an excellent job with the publishing house, increasing the paid circulation of the church's monthly magazine, *The Voice of Glory*, from less than 2000 subscribers to nearly 100,000. Furthermore, he made their trade journal, *Eye On The Sparrow*, the publication of choice for articles of leading gospel scholars in the country, and made their monthly children's magazine very popular with the children of the church.

Most of all, the department published all the religious tracts authored by Bishop Crombie, Sr. himself, including a Bible doctrine book. Since the publishing house was the pride and joy of the church, and because it was very profitable, everyone pretty much left it alone, including Bishop Hazelton, who gave his nephew's financial reports and records only scant attention when they were turned in to him.

Years later when Bishop Hazelton died, Bishop Tom Jr. assigned his daughter Viola the job of overseeing the publishing department. It wasn't that anything was amiss. It was only that Rev. C.P. Hazelton was very ambitious in his publishing plans, and Bishop Tom Jr. felt that he might be moving too fast.

"Rev. Hazelton's doing a fine job, but he wants us to do a little trade publishing. He's even lined up a few retail outlets, and has begun soliciting manuscripts from authors. I think he might be moving too fast. I want you to keep an eye on things, Viola," he charged his daughter, who after graduating from the seminary was pastoring her own church at the time. She hadn't yet met and married Albert Flowers.

At her father's direction she took over jurisdiction of the publishing department, but tried to stay out of Rev. C.P. Hazelton's way as much as possible. As Rev. Hazelton's uncle had done before her, she largely gave him free rein, and, save a few minor disagreements over some large purchase orders, the two of them got along quite well.

Then one day while going through some old financial records of the publishing department, Viola came across some billings that smelled fishy. In fact very fishy. The documents went back years. They were records that Bishop Hazelton had probably filed away without really looking at them.

"I think we should bring in an accountant to examine these records, Daddy. I don't know much about accounting, but some of these old bills don't look right, particularly some of the printing bills," she told her father, giving him a disquieting look.

She disliked having to take such troubling news to her father about a person like Rev. C. P. Hazelton who had become very powerful and respected in the church. Because her father was the kind of person who gave everyone the benefit of the doubt, she knew she had to have all of her facts right.

Her father looked at her in disbelief, thinking she was exaggerating. He too was a supporter of Rev. C.P. Hazelton for the good job he had done with the publishing department. In fact he had given Rev. Hazelton many raises over the years for the commendable job he was doing.

Seeing the doubt on her father's face, she showed him some of the records that bothered her, pointing out the discrepancies.

"But some of these records are nearly twenty years old," he said as he tried hard to find an excuse to dismiss what he was seeing. The import of what his daughter was suggesting was very disturbing. "Does Viola realize what she's doing?" he asked himself with a long face. The records she was showing him, if really evidence of what she was claiming, could send Rev. Hazelton to prison for years.

Seeing the befuddlement on his face, she said, "That's the point, Daddy. It goes back all those years and it's still going on." She removed more records from her briefcase and showed him some of a recent date.

Wide-eyed he examined the records. He grimaced painfully as the unthinkable became thinkable. He was thinking of Bishop Hazelton, the man who made him presiding bishop. Because of all the senior bishops who wanted the position, he would have never gotten the job without Bishop Hazelton's help. Now he might have to bring criminal charges against a person Bishop Hazelton loved like a son.

With a sad face, he got up from his desk as more unthinkable thoughts entered his mind. He mumbled something to himself. He looked like someone who had just taken a big dose of castor oil.

He rubbed his chin in thought and frowned. Come to think of it, he had always wondered how Rev. Hazelton was able to live so well on what they paid him. Rev. C.P. Hazelton owned the largest, most expensive home in the Negro section of town, and he bought a big new car every year.

He told Viola grimly, "Continue with your investigation, honey, but keep it under your hat. And proceed with discretion. I'm sure Rev. Hazelton can satisfactorily explain all of this." He wanted to drop to his knees and pray that Rev. Hazelton indeed had satisfactory answers.

In the meantime Rev. C. P. Hazelton had become suspicious that he was being investigated. The owner of the paper company where the church did business called him about the young black lady minister who was asking questions about his billings. "Who is she? She's asking me questions about transactions that go back nearly twenty years. I had to spend the whole weekend down in the basement pulling out all that old stuff. What's going on, Reverend?" the white man asked concerned.

The church's typesetting company voiced the same complaint.

The information that Viola was unearthing was beginning to show that Rev. C. P. Hazelton had gotten big kickbacks all those years.

"Oh my!" she gasped when it fully hit her what was happening.

Chapter Twenty-one

Then before Viola's investigation was finished, Bishop Tom Jr. suddenly died. His death shocked everyone. Viola was devastated, for she loved her father dearly. The funeral was one of the saddest in the history of the church. This was a very difficult period for Viola Crombie. Adding to her family woes was the unfinished Rev. Hazelton matter.

After her father's burial, the battle over who would succeed him as presiding bishop began immediately. His body was still warm in the grave; Viola didn't even have time to grieve. In the minds of most in the General Assembly, despite her young age, she was the leading candidate to get her father's job. Then a powerful clique of dissidents organized quickly to stop her. Some of the people in the clique opposed her because she was female.

"A woman has no business heading the church. It's bad enough that we ordain them and allow them to preach," one disgruntled male bishop said when opposing her.

His group was a small minority. The Church of God & Spirit had never had a bar against women entering the ministry. Rev. Viola Crombie was very proud of her grandfather for leading the movement in the founding days of their church that welcomed female ministers from the very beginning. His enlightened position on the women question was far ahead of the times, even in the white world.

The few girls attending the seminary with Viola were there largely against the wishes of their parents who had tried to dissuade them from entering the ministry. Those parents saw the ministry as no place for a female, which wasn't the case with Viola Crombie. She attended the seminary with the full blessing of her parents who saw nothing wrong with a woman being a preacher. This belief was in line with her church's tradition that her grandfather had helped establish.

A few bishops opposed her because they wanted the job of presiding bishop for themselves. One such bishop was Bishop Fox who felt at long last his time had come to head the national church.

He missed that opportunity once, and he didn't want that to happen again. Years ago when Viola's grandfather died, Bishop Fox backed Bishop Hazelton for the job over her father. "I think you should succeed Bishop Crombie, Bishop Hazelton. You're next in line. You served Bishop Crombie longer than any of us," he said to Bishop Hazelton at the time.

But Bishop Hazelton declined the position. Besides his promise to Bishop Crombie regarding Rev. Tom Jr., Bishop Hazelton didn't want the job because he felt he was too old. "The clock's against me," he told Bishop Fox.

Although no spring chicken himself, as third-in-command of the church, Bishop Fox wanted the job if Bishop Hazelton didn't want it. "If you don't want the job, Bishop Hazelton, then I'll take it. Damn it, I deserve it—after you, I'm next in line. I helped build this church, too," he bewailed against the idea of young Tom Jr. being picked ahead of him.

Whereupon he threw his hat in the ring and a messy succession fight ensued. But Bishop Fox's meager forces were no match for Bishop Hazelton's and Rev. Tom Jr.'s massive forces. Rev. Tom Jr. won handily and became the new presiding bishop of the church.

That was some years ago. Now even older, feebler, and on a cane, Bishop Fox still wanted his chance to head the church. This time around he aligned himself with one of the most powerful people in the church, Rev. C.P. Hazelton. Because of his role in the church's publishing business, Rev. C.P. Hazelton had become almost as powerful as a bishop. Many clergymen and church scholars curried favor with him to get their articles published, and many feared the power of his printing presses.

Some bishops even looked to him for leadership, particularly the disgruntled ones. Since Rev. C.P. Hazelton believed that Rev. Viola Crombie was out to get him, he hated her. He feared she would expose his bilking schemes, and felt he had to discredit her before she destroyed him. So he backed Bishop Fox in a campaign that turned out to be the dirtiest and bloodiest fight in church history. His forces in the church began attacking Rev. Flowers even before she was nominated.

Believing she was too young for such a responsible position, Viola didn't want the job of presiding bishop. Therefore, she withdrew her name from nomination, and backed a friend of her father's, the bishop of the Midwest District whom she had known and admired since she was a small girl. She liked and respected Bishop Fox, but felt he was too old for the job. The church was expanding rapidly, and needed younger, more energetic leadership that could keep up with the times, she felt.

Although she and her supporters succeeded in getting their candidate nominated by the Executive Board, they lost in the General Assembly, because at the eleventh hour all of the church's publications endorsed Bishop Fox. This was a historical first for the church, for in the past the publishing department stayed out of elections. When Viola's candidate failed to get the necessary votes to get confirmed in the General Assembly, the dissidents cleverly nominated Bishop Fox from the floor of the General Assembly, where a vote was taken and the old man won. Bishop Fox finally became presiding bishop of the church.

Rev. Viola Crombie was the first person to congratulate him on his victory. She promised him her full support, and she sincerely meant it, for she had nothing against him personally. She had opposed him only because of his advanced age. He had served both her grandfather and father well as a top officer in the church. When she was a small child he had bounced her on his knee.

He likewise held no ill-feelings towards her. "I'm sorry I had to oppose you, Viola. I'm sure you understand that it wasn't personal. I'm an old man. I won't be around long. It'll be your turn soon enough," he told her in their first meeting after the election. Despite that she had removed herself from the race long before the process began, he spoke to her as if she had been the candidate who had run against him.

The battle for the presiding bishop post had been very bruising. Had the contestants been prizefighters, both boxers would have been hospitalized. The church now needed to heal, Viola felt. She hoped the wounds weren't as deep as all the bleeding suggested. After praying on it for nearly a week, she decided the only way the church could come together again was for her to leave the church. She reasoned that since she had been the main person the dissidents had passionately opposed, it should be her who departed. Many of the attacks against her were ad hominem, with some even bringing up her past love affair with Rev. Scott, a minister of another denomination.

The decision to pull up stakes and move to California was very painful for her. She loved the church that her beloved grandfather had built from scratch. She loved all the people in the church. She loved the fact that it was also her father's church. That Bishop Fox offered to make her the bishop of her district made the decision even more agonizing. But for sake of the church she had to leave; she felt she had no other choice.

However, before she left she had to dispose of the "Rev. Hazelton Affair." She told Bishop Fox in private about what she and her father had discovered about Rev. Hazelton's bilking scheme. She turned all her evidence over to him, and the old bishop, an honest man, was flabbergasted.

"The accountant Daddy hired has all the details. I'll pray for the Lord to give you the wisdom and courage to handle this matter, Bishop Fox," she said as she turned and left him standing there speechless.

She knew Bishop Fox was a good man and would do what was necessary to protect the church, notwithstanding that Rev. Hazelton was his chief backer. She also knew Bishop Fox would want her to stay on and help him resolved the matter, so she left quickly before he could make that request. Her being around when the "Rev. Hazelton Affair" became public would only aggravate matters, she figured.

She hurried home, packed her things, and moved to California, where she established her own church that she left unaffiliated. In California she met and married Albert Flowers.

Chapter Twenty-two

On the day after the Midwest Conference ended, Rev. Flowers went to dinner with her old friend Betty Harris, whom she had spent scant time with due to the rush of the conference. Betty now lived in St. Louis where the Harris family moved to when Viola and Betty were in high school, which was the second saddest day in Viola's life.

The saddest day in her life was the day when she learned that her other best childhood friend, Irene Radnick, had died. One day nine-year-old Viola Crombie decided to go to the Radnick home to check on Irene, since Irene hadn't come around in nearly two weeks. Normally Irene visited Viola nearly every day. Viola had called her repeatedly, but no one answered the telephone at the Radnick home.

As often happens with children, Viola's concern regarding Irene quickly enlarged into fear. Fear that Irene had moved away without telling her. The last time Viola saw her Czech friend, Irene's mother and father had had a big fight, and Irene's mother had threatened to move out and take the children with her. The Radnicks fought constantly. Over the years Mrs. Radnick threatened repeatedly to leave Mr. Radnick, but she never did.

"We're not moving anywhere. Mama only says that to get Daddy to stop drinking," young Irene told Viola one day in that matter-of-fact way of hers.

This time, however, Viola feared Irene's mother had acted on her threat. Viola had a feeling in the hollow of her stomach that something was drastically wrong. "People can take only so much," Viola's mother would say when hearing news that someone they knew had snapped and gotten into trouble.

Young Viola knew as a reality of life that families often break up and move away. The Lauder family came vividly to mind. The Lauders, a black family who lived down the block from them in Iowa, fought constantly and the police was always at their front door. Once little Viola saw the police remove Mr. Lauder from the Lauder home in handcuffs and take him away in a squad car. This happened often. Then one day after a big fight, while Mr. Lauder was still in jail, Mrs. Lauder packed up their four kids, loaded them into a yellow cab and hurried to the Greyhound bus station, and left on the first bus she could get out of town. She didn't even bother to close the front door to their house when she left. The house stood there for nearly a week, full of clothes, furniture and other personal things, with the front door wide open to the street. It was very eerie. The house stood exposed like a shivering naked person until a neighbor mercifully ventured over, shut the door, and secured things until Mr. Lauder got out of jail.

Young Viola also remembered the Fosters who used to live across the street from her. Mr. Foster had escaped from an Indiana prison and had made a new life for himself in Cherry Bluffs under a different name. While at large he happily married a local girl and they had three nice children. He was a highly respected citizen of the neighborhood. One day the police arrested him while he was entertaining some friends at his home. The family moved away in what seemed like only days after he was extradited to Indiana.

Therefore, Viola knew families suddenly moved for all kinds of reasons. In her young mind she was now sure that Irene's mother had moved suddenly without giving Irene a chance to notify her. Nearly in tears Viola had to go and see for herself.

On her way to Irene's house, as she passed the Catholic Church that Irene attended, she saw a procession of cars lined up behind a big black hearse. People dressed in black were coming out of the church. Then some men came out carrying a small casket that they put into the hearse. Looking on in the crowd on the sidewalk, Viola saw Irene's family, also dressed in black, sobbing. She looked for Irene among them, then it painfully dawned on her—Irene was in the casket.

"Oh Viola! Irene's gone!" Irene's mother wailed when she spied Viola among the onlookers. She flung her white arms open like a wide cape and hugged the black child. "I'm sorry! I'm so sorry!" she apologized profusely to Viola for forgetting to tell her about Irene's death. She realized what she had done was unforgivable, because the two girls were best friends. Later Viola learned Irene died from acute appendicitis.

After Irene Radnick died, Viola and Betty Harris became even closer.

In St. Louis Viola looked at Betty sitting across from her in the restaurant, and regretted that Betty and Irene never became close friends. She glanced at her watch. "I hadn't realized it was so late. I must get back to the hotel. I have an early flight to Atlanta in the morning."

"Please stay for a few more days, Vi. You can stay with me. I'll prepare the guest room for you. We have so much more to talk about," Betty begged her old friend; in her head Betty had already planned a dozen things for them to do tomorrow.

Viola chuckled sadly, "I wish I could Betty, but I must keep traveling. Discount plane tickets don't allow much flexibility." It was needless for her to remind Betty that ministers didn't make much money.

Rev. Flowers didn't relish continuing on to Georgia where she had heard the temperature today was nearly 100 degrees in the shade. But she had to make the trip. The mystery of the Bible was still gnawing at her like a stubborn rat chewing through a burlap bag of corn. She had mentioned the Bustersons to Betty who agreed with Lettie that it was probably just a hand-me-down Bible and was nothing to worry about. "Some people don't mind using secondhand things. Some do it because they can't afford anything better. Some do it because they're just cheap," Betty said.

Then she laughed, "Speaking of cheap, my brother and sister-in-law don't believe in throwing anything away. My sister-in-law uses the same piece of aluminum foil over and over again. After she uses a piece, she washes it with her dishes. She won't throw it in the trash unless it begins to crack and fall apart. She hasn't bought a new roll of Reynolds Wrap in years. Whenever I ask her about it, she says, 'Girl, aluminum foil's made to be recycled.'

Betty added, "It isn't that she and Hughie are poor. They both have good jobs and make plenty of money. It's just that they're cheap. Their kitchen drawers are crammed with discount coupons of all kinds. Hughie has this elaborate computer program that allows him to keep track of all their coupons, even the expiration dates. Before they do their weekly shopping he runs their weekly shopping list through the computer and punches up all the coupons they will need for their trip to the store. 'Coupons only make sense when they save you money on items you really need. Otherwise, they waste money,' Hughie says."

Betty shook her head and let out a big laugh, "Child, those two are so cheap that they would reuse their toilet paper if they could find a way to do it."

Chapter Twenty-three

It was the early 1900s in Dougherty County. While most black farmers in the Deep South were sharecroppers, the Bustersons owned their small 140-acre cotton farm. Sam Busterson bought the farm, acre by acre, with the extra money he earned by hiring himself out to the large white plantations in the area. Because he was so handy with tools and machines, he got all the extra work he wanted. White people liked and trusted him.

But his own farm always came first. While most black farmers used mules, he always worked with horses. In fact he had a good eye for strong, intelligent work animals. He believed that although mules were cheaper to acquire and maintain, you could earn more money with a horse. "You can do so much more with a good plow horse than you can with a good mule. The difference in price is worth it," he advised his sons.

He and his oldest son Tom often attended horse auctions, always the only black faces there. Even though the auctions were "White Only," whites allowed Sam Busterson to participate because, not only did they like him, but they knew that sometimes in the future they might need his help with something. At the time Sam Busterson was the closest thing to a county farm agent that they had. He knew just about everything about farming, from the medical treatment of animals, the repair of machinery, to the care of the soil. He was the first farmer in the area to rotate his crops on a regular basis. His small farm produced more per acre than any farm in the county, and he never had trouble with boll weevils.

At the auctions Sam Busterson would bid on animals he wanted with the ferocity of a wealthy art dealer. With their mouths open and eyes gaping, the Negro workers at the auction would stare in disbelief at this bold black man aggressively bidding with white men like he was one of them. He was so good at getting bargains at auctions that he always kept a few horses, mules, and cows on his farm to sell or trade if the right deal came along. He made money at it. And he taught his son Tom how to be good at business as well.

Sam Busterson was a very fugal man. He regularly went to the county dump in his horse and wagon to hunt for things of value that wealthy white people had thrown away. He would retrieve them from the dump, load them into his wagon, take them home, clean them up, and repair them if required. He would use the things himself or store them in the barn to be sold later.

"You can find some good stuff in here. It's unbelievable the good things white folks throw away," he would tell his sons while they rummaged through the trash and garbage.

He and his two sons often went to the dump for target practice. With their .22 rifles in hand, they would select a good spot and shoot the rats they spied slinking in the garbage of the dump. "This is good target practice for shooting rats around the barn. Boys, do you know how much grain one family of rats can destroy? Rats can wipe out all your profit. They are fast breeders, and they'll put you in the poor farm if you don't keep them under control. I believe a rifle or shotgun is better than poison," he would tell his sons.

Sam Busterson was a deeply religious man who worked hard for the sake of his children. His dream was to build something he could pass down to them. His father, who died a weary and broken-down man at an early age from sharecropping worthless land all his life, left his family nothing but debts. Sam Busterson swore that would not happen to him. He tried to teach his children all he knew so they could have a better life.

His oldest son Tom hung on his father's every word as though spoken by God. Tom was a very smart and mirthlessly serious young man, who was never without his Bible. "Lillian, that boy's going to be a preacher someday," Sam would say proudly to his wife about how their son would study his Bible whenever he had a chance. At night by the light of the kerosene lamp, Tom could be found reading the Bible to his siblings. Even way back then, he claimed the Lord often spoke to him.

Tom was the son Sam Busterson depended on to look after the family if anything happened to him. Rufus, the younger son, was just the opposite. He seemed born only to play and have fun, and later when he was older, only to fight, gamble, and run after women. His other child, the youngest, was a daughter who was extremely intelligent but very withdrawn. She seemed to live in a world of her own.

One day Sam Busterson and his son Tom hired on with a lumber company to earn some extra money. The first day on the job Sam was killed by a falling tree. Now the full burden of the family was on young Tom's broad shoulders. He turned out to be a harder worker than even his father. Unlike his father who was a man known for his sense of humor and cheerful disposition, Tom Busterson seldom joked or smiled. He felt that God found Man's frivolity displeasing. In addition to being a farmer, he became a preacher, saying the Lord commanded him to do so. "I'm at your service, O Lord," he replied at the time of his ordination, with tears of joy rolling down his cheeks.

He built his first church with his own hands from the logs he cut down in the woods.

****

Tom Busterson farmed days and pastored nights and on Sundays, and was successful at both. He continued buying and selling at auctions as his father had done so successfully. Without a doubt he was the most eligible Negro bachelor in that part of Georgia. Every Negro family in the county wanted this single, hardworking young man as a son-in-law. Parents schemed to help their daughter catch his eye. Teenage girls of the church vied for his attention. But young Rev. Tom Busterson had no room in his life for romance. He had room only for God, his family, and his farm and business.

One Sunday while preaching the Sunday sermon, he looked down from the pulpit and saw this beautiful angel sitting in the pews. A gorgeous brown-skinned girl of about seventeen or eighteen he hadn't seen before. Her black curly hair was done up with red ribbons, and her large brown eyes sparkled like beautiful diamonds. He was smitten with her. He was sure God had sent her to him, and that she was why he had waited and practiced celibacy. As he looked down at her, tears of appreciation filled his eyes. He reached for the sky and silently thanked the Lord.

The pretty Negro girl sitting in the congregation was not an angel. Far from it. She was seventeen-year-old Fannie Mae Higgins from Atlanta. And she wasn't visiting. Unbeknownst to the young reverend, she had been sent to Florenceville to live with relatives by order of a juvenile court in Atlanta. The kindly old white judge at her sentencing flipped through her probation report and then looked up and said to her, "I see here that you have a very high IQ. With an intelligence like that, you should be trying to make something of yourself. You should be in school preparing to help your people."

By "your people," he meant the Negro people. He gazed down at her with a fatherly look on his face. He too was enraptured by that angelic quality of hers. By that pretty face and those big bright eyes that turned things they looked at into mush. He couldn't believe that she was arrested with Atlanta's most notorious Negro gambler, a man known for his crooked crap and card games. A man known for slicing up other men in gambling disputes with that straight razor he kept hidden in his stocking tops. On the night she was arrested with him, he killed a man over some marked cards. While the probation report said she was his girlfriend and had assisted him in the cheating, it pointed out that due to her young age she was probably taken advantage of by the much older man.

Moved by the sympathetic probation report, the judge gave her the choice of either going to the state reformatory or leaving town. "Since age twelve, you've done nothing but get into trouble with the law. Since age twelve, your parents have had trouble with you. For most of your teenage years, you've run around with the wrong crowd. Against my better judgment, I'm going to give you one last chance. Go live with your aunt in Florenceville and make something of yourself. The probation report says your aunt is willing to help you. Or go to jail for a long time. The choice is yours, young lady."

She chose to live with her aunt in Florenceville.

On the Sunday morning when Rev. Busterson first saw her, Fannie Mae Higgins was attending church with her aunt and uncle and their children. Wanting to stay in her aunt and uncle's good graces, she had spruced herself up for church, wearing the prettiest dress she owned. Even without makeup she was stunning, and the teenage boys and young men at church couldn't take their eyes off her. In fact she made all the men in the congregation very uncomfortable. And young Rev. Busterson was no exception.

Although she sat there demurely minding her own business, she smiled inwardly with deep satisfaction, for she realized how she was affecting the males in the congregation, even the young boys. More important, she could see how nervous the young pastor was. Several times she caught him stealing looks at her like a bashful teenager. She smiled to herself when her bold eyes caused his timid eyes to run and hide. "Naughty, naughty," her bold eyes scolded him playfully. She too knew what a terrific catch he would be for any woman.

Rev. Busterson was a very fair man. His father had taught him that a man's word was his bond. His strong sense of fairness was why he did so well in the horse-trading business left him by his father that made him the most prosperous Negro bachelor in the county. If after a sale one of his animals was found to be crippled or infirm, Tom Busterson would gladly take it back and make a full refund. As was true with his father, people could rely on his warranties.

When the Higgins girl asked about him after church that first day, her Aunt Leeza said sternly, "Fannie Mae, you leave Rev. Busterson alone. You hear me. You're here to stay out of trouble, not start trouble." Her aunt's reproach only made her more interested in the handsome young clergyman. Sunday after Sunday her flirting with him became more outrageous.

****

One evening there was a knock on Aunt Leeza's door. There stood Rev. Tom Busterson, all dressed up with a bouquet of flowers in one hand and a small beribboned gift in the other. He asked for Fannie Mae, who was called to the door. He gave Fannie Mae the gift and flowers, who kept the gift, but handed her Aunt Leeza the flowers.

"What is it?" Fannie Mae asked about the gift, fingering it curiously. Outwardly she tried to be blasé about the small package, but inwardly she was hoping it was jewelry. Aunt Leeza took the flowers and put them in water, while Fannie Mae stood there pondering the small brightly wrapped package.

"Open it," Rev Busterson said as he grinned broadly.

She opened it and found a small leather-covered, gold embossed prayer book. It was a thing of beauty.

"I'd like you to come to our Bible classes on Thursday nights. I think you'd find them enjoyable. I teach the class myself."

That night in bed Aunt Leeza turned to her husband and lamented to him, "Wilbur, what have we done?" She was referring to Fannie Mae and Rev. Busterson. She and her husband were both members of his church, and they knew what a good and religious man he was. He had always been a person of God, even when a small boy when he carried his Bible with him wherever he went.

On the other hand, they knew what a troublemaker Fannie Mae could be. Since age twelve she had nearly driven her mother in Atlanta insane with worry. All the court appearances over the years on Fannie Mae's behalf had turned Leeza's sister's hair prematurely gray. Leeza knew Fannie Mae could be disastrous to a good man like Rev. Busterson. She was so strong-willed and uncontrollable. Even at twelve, she was a feral cat.

"Maybe this is a part of God's plan," Leeza's husband Wilbur tried to comfort his wife. "You said yourself that Fannie Mae has a big heart. Maybe it's God's will that she pairs up with a strong moral man like Rev. Busterson. A man who can control her and help her build a new life. A man who can introduce her to God."

Aunt Leeza got out of bed that night and got down on her knees and prayed that Wilbur was right.

****

Fannie Mae's Aunt Leeza and Uncle Wilbur were not the only ones who worried about Rev. Busterson. Florenceville was a small town, and secrets are hard to keep in small towns. One person tells another person a secret, and soon the whole town knows it. A few weeks after Fannie Mae arrived in Florenceville with her tattered suitcase, the whole town knew about her criminal past in Atlanta, including the Busterson family. Rev. Busterson saw Fannie Mae as both a blessing and a challenge.

Soon the entire town buzzed about how Fannie Mae was beguiling the minister.

****

A few months later Rev. Busterson proposed, and Fannie Mae

quickly accepted his offer of marriage. Rev. Busterson's widowed mother was very upset about it. "Tom, you're not being sensible about this. That wild girl is not the kind of person a minister should have for a wife."

"Shame on you, Ma. You're a Christian, and good Christians should believe in redemption. Paul said to the Corinthians that if any man be in Christ, he is a new creature. Old things are passed away. Behold, all things are now new. Fannie Mae is now in Christ, and is a new creature of the Lord."

Dutifully holding her tongue, Rev. Busterson's old mother fought back the tears and accepted her son's wishes. It was the saddest day of her life.

Chapter Twenty-four

Rev. Tom Busterson would curse the day he met that girl. His consuming love for her made Fannie Mae behave like a spoiled brat. Once they were married she began tormenting him unlike anything he had experienced before in his life. In fact it began even before they married.

At her first session in Bible class, Fannie Mae started boldly challenging his interpretation of scripture in front of the class. At first it made the class interesting. She was very intelligent with a mind like a bear trap. Little escaped from it. Her questions were sharp and to the point, and her presence made the others, especially the young men, sit up straight in their chairs and listen. At first young Rev. Busterson used her questioning him as a Socratic teaching device to clarify points or provide illustrations or drive discussion of the subject matter. After all, she was a young rebel sent to him by God so he could save her soul.

With time, her challenging him became more vicious; she started mocking him. She seemed to delight in the power she had over him and liked making him squirm. The mocking in class, sometimes even in public, really began after she started taunting him in bed over his lousy lovemaking. "Lousy" was her term. According to her, he couldn't do anything right in bed. Under their warm comforter at night, when she wasn't blaming him for being too clumsy, or too rough, or too inapt, or for ejaculating too quickly, she blamed him generally for failing to satisfy her sexually.

"I've been with fourteen-year-old boys who fucked better than you. You're pathetic!" she would scream at him before hopping out of bed when they were done like a whore with an urgent appointment to be somewhere else. She would rush into the bathroom and wash up like she couldn't wait another second to get his awful sweat and odor off of her.

Every time that happened it nearly destroyed him. When Fannie Mae returned to their big brass bed and pulled the covers up over her head like a tent and dropped off to sleep, he would lie there in the dark and silently ask God what had he done wrong. Sometimes he was nearly in tears.

He knew she might have had a legitimate basis for complaining. Having practiced celibacy all his life, he knew next to nothing about carnal lovemaking. Because of his religion, he would have burned the Kama Sutra had he known about the book in his day. Oddly, though, he was very knowledgeable about animal husbandry. He believed that animals having sex was natural, beautiful, and essential, and decreed by God. He preferred not to watch them, however, because of the strange feelings he always got when he did so, a dirty feeling he ascribed to the work of the Devil. Thus his only guides to sex were his barnyard animals, particularly his horses. The stallion mounted the mare and then—amain!—it was all over. Sex seemed so simple when animals did it.

Fannie Mae took to flirting with every man in the church she found attractive, even the married ones, and was very brazen about it. With those big soulful eyes, she could send messages of seduction as effectively as a telegraph machine. Then there was that seductive walk of hers. Women of the church would snatch their husbands by the arm and quickly move away when they saw her coming their way. She made everyone uncomfortable. Some sisters in the church even accused her of flirting with some of the females.

To get her to behave like a minister's wife should, young Rev. Tom Busterson would lavish Fannie Mae with expensive gifts, often things he couldn't really afford. It would work for awhile. Like a naughty little girl around Christmas time she would apologize and promise to change. "It isn't easy being a preacher's wife. You have to bite your tongue, and I'm used to saying what's on my mind. Also, most of those old fogies are so boring," she would pout cutely, whereupon he would hurry out and buy her another pretty gift. All that gift buying put a strain on his finances.

Then on Sundays Rev. Busterson began noticing a strange young man all dressed up who would come in after the service had begun, and sit in the rear of the church near the door. At first Rev. Busterson didn't give him much thought. There were many black men on the road in those days, some walking from town to town looking for work, some hoboing in on freight trains. In those days people hopped empty boxcars the same as people hop buses today. Deacon Brown of their church, for instance, had a peg leg because one day when hopping a freight train to Atlanta to visit relatives, his grip on the train gave way, and he fell under the wheels of the train and lost his leg. Now he joked about it.

On Sundays many black hobos would head for the first Negro church they could find, since they knew they wouldn't be stoned at a black church. Some black men on the road came to church because they missed their families, and church was where they went on Sundays when at home. Others simply wanted to be with black worshipers on Sundays. Some came because they were hungry, and usually some religious family would take them home for dinner afterwards. Others came because, just passing through town, they didn't have anywhere else to go where dogs wouldn't be sicced on them. In those hostile times, the Negro Church was the lighthouse that beckoned poor black men on the road.

But this strange man was different. For one thing, he was younger. Most of the traveling men that Rev. Busterson was accustomed to seeing were older men out on the road trying to find work to support their families. Many were older men running from the law, or older men trying to pick up their lives after just being released from prison. Some were traveling musicians trying to earn a living. Some were tramps just knocking around the country. The younger men were usually farm boys escaping the hard knocks of Southern rural life.

This young man fitted none of those descriptions. He was about twenty-two, nattily dressed, and wore highly polished shoes. He had a certain urbanity about him that suggested the night life of New Orleans or Atlanta. He had a smirk on his good-looking face of someone in on a plan. In fact he seemed to be there on a mission. Because of the young man's confident air, the cocky way he crossed his legs and extended his arms along the back of the pew, Rev. Busterson at first thought he might be a traveling salesman. He had that cocky way about him. But Sundays were the wrong days of the week for traveling salesmen, most of whom were home on Sundays.

Every Sunday after the service was over, Rev. Busterson would rush to the door of the church so he could meet and shake hands with the stranger, but every week by the time he got there, the man was gone. One congregant told him that he believed the young man was from Rocklin County, a county over from theirs. Rev. Busterson gave the man no further thought.

One Sunday from the pulpit Rev. Busterson noticed that the congregation had become very restive. They were behaving like skittish deer that had sensed a predator nearby. At first Rev. Busterson thought that maybe a snake had gotten into the church, since there were snakes in the weeds outside. Then he noticed that the church members' attention was not on him in the pulpit, but was alternating between the young stranger in the back of the church and Fannie Mae sitting in her pew in front of the church. The two young people were brazenly exchanging eye and face messages. There was much whispering among the congregation. Still Rev. Busterson in his naivety didn't comprehend what was going on in the pews.

One Sunday what everyone feared happened. In the middle of Rev. Busterson's sermon, his wife Fannie Mae rose from her seat and the young stranger got to his feet, and the two of them pranced out of the church, arm and arm, like high school sweethearts. When outside, Fannie Mae and the young man howled with laughter like they had just pulled off the prank of the century.

The entire congregation, including the children, looked on in utter disbelief, while Rev. Busterson just stood there frozen in place like an ice carving.

The two young people disappeared into the woods and neither of them was ever seen alive again.

Chapter Twenty-five

Aunt Jennie suggested to Rev. Flowers that her first stop in Georgia should be the Peach Crescent Nursing Home where Aunt Belle died, so she could speak to the staff members who took care of Aunt Belle when she was alive. It was Aunt Jennie who signed Aunt Belle into the nursing home. Once when visiting Aunt Belle when she was still living alone on her acreage, Aunt Jennie noticed how erratic Aunt Belle's driving had become. This cause her to have deep concern.

Aunt Belle had owned automobiles for years. She loved to drive and was very expert at it. Even when she reached her eighties she continued to take long road trips alone, once driving all the way to Branson, Missouri, to see some shows. In fact she was among the first motorists in the state to be licensed. She loved telling the story about when she was stopped for speeding in 1937 by a young man just hired in Georgia's first batch of state troopers. "The young man still had the price tag on his new uniform. I told him about the tag and helped him remove it," she was fond of telling people.

"Aunt Belle was a good driver. I always felt safe with her behind the wheel. Then she started driving recklessly, which wasn't like her," Aunt Jennie told Viola Flowers one day on the phone, "Once when she and I were going to Wal-Mart for something or another, she wrongfully made a left-hand turn into oncoming traffic of a divided highway. We could've been killed. Thank goodness there wasn't any traffic coming toward us, so we were able to turn around safely and get out of there. It didn't faze Aunt Belle a bit. While I nearly had a heart attack, she was very blasé about it. She didn't see what all the fuss was about. That same day we had a couple of other near misses."

In that telephone call Aunt Jennie's tone became very dire, as was the rest of her story. "For the first time I noticed how much her ability to get around had diminished. When I returned home, I started looking into nursing homes in her area, just in case she got so bad that she should be put in a home."

A few months later Aunt Jennie told Viola that Aunt Belle's condition had gotten worse. "Aunt Belle is a danger in the kitchen. She puts a pot on the stove to heat something up or places something in the oven to bake, and then forgets it's there. Several times she nearly burned her house down. Whenever I visit her, I'm afraid to leave her there alone. It reached a point where I had to speak to her about how she was placing her life in danger by living alone. She refused to listen to any talk about her going into an old folks' home. Please talk to her, Viola. Maybe she'll listen to you," she told Viola on one of her long-distance calls.

Viola remembered that call, and she did talk to Aunt Belle about it, who merely laughed and accused Aunt Jennie of being a worrywart.

After that occasion Viola Flowers and Aunt Jennie had many long-distance telephone conversations about Aunt Belle's living alone. Then one day Aunt Jennie called her and said, "Yesterday out of the clear blue Aunt Belle called me and asked me to come down when I could and take her around to look at some nursing homes in her town. It seemed that for no apparent reason she started fainting. And that she stayed dizzy all the time. At first the doctors thought it was just the side effects of Aunt Bell's medicines, but changing the prescriptions didn't improve things any. She continued to pass out at the strangest times. She told me that one afternoon she was lying on her sofa reading when the UPS man knocked on her door. She got up and opened the door, and the next thing she knew she was flat on her back on the floor looking up at the startled white man who was frightened to death. She said she didn't think she lost consciousness."

Aunt Jennie continued, "She told me about another time when she got up in the middle of the night to go to the bathroom. Then when getting up from the toilet she fainted and collapsed to the floor, badly bruising her knees and shoulder. It was a miracle that she didn't fracture her hip like so many old people do when going to the toilet in the middle of the night. This frightened her terribly."

Aunt Jennie then said, "Being a nurse herself Aunt Belle realized her danger. I begged her to come and live with me, but she didn't want to be a burden and insisted on going into a nursing home. She chose the Peach Crescent Nursing Home, which was in her price range and was where many of her old patients were staying."

When she got off the airplane in Georgia, Viola Flowers went directly to Aunt Jennie's home, where Aunt Jennie told her, "The young nurse's assistant who took care of Aunt Belle said that in the last days of her life, Aunt Belle sobbed constantly and prattled senselessly about someone being brutally murdered. The medical staff said it was like Aunt Belle's mental faculties had deteriorated almost overnight. The last time I visited her she was fine."

"Brutally murdered?" Viola Flowers gasped.

"Yes. It was probably just foolish babble, but it won't hurt to look into it."

And this was what Rev. Flowers did; her next stop was Aunt Belle's nursing home.

****

Although located in the heart of town, the Peach Crescent Nursing Home was set back from the street, nearly hidden in the magnolia trees. It was a less than two hour drive from Aunt Jennie's home. Before becoming a nursing home, the old Victorian house, with its tall stately white columns and sweeping verandas, was formerly the mansion of the town's most prominent family. Now shabby and peeling, it was only a pitiful shadow of its former self. In the afternoon the old folks, some in wheelchairs, sat out on the veranda and enjoyed the breeze from the park next door. Aunt Belle loved sitting in her room in her rocking chair and watching the beautiful butterflies flitting amid the blossoms on the peach and cherry trees outside her window.

The staff member who knew Aunt Belle the best was a young white lady attending college days and working at the nursing home in the evenings. Despite that she had other patients in her charge, she and Aunt Belle became very close. Aunt Belle encouraged her in her studies, and advised her on her personal problems. Aunt Belle also defeated her at checkers more times than not. Although accustomed to patients dying, the young attendant was especially saddened by Aunt Belle's death.

Rev. Flowers spoke to the young attendant first. The two of them took seats at the far end of the veranda so they could talk in private. Rev. Flowers didn't know how to start the conversation. "I understand my aunt became very disoriented around the time of her death," she began with great delicacy.

The young attendant's blue eyes saddened. "It happened very suddenly. One day your aunt was doing just fine, then the very next day she became this hysterical person who couldn't stop crying and tormenting herself about something she believed happened in her childhood."

"What things in her childhood?" Rev. Flowers queried nervously.

"The doctor said your aunt probably lost her grip on reality, and became this terrified child trapped in a nightmare from which she couldn't escape. Old people often lose their hold on reality and slide off into some other world. He didn't think what she said had any basis in reality."

"Are you saying my aunt had Alzheimer?"

"We don't really know. It happened so fast. Because of her advanced age the doctor didn't recommend an autopsy. It might have been a brain tumor of some kind."

"You said she talked about being involved in a murder. Did she say who was murdered?"

"Nothing was really intelligible. It was mostly disconnected ramblings about her early childhood here in Georgia. She talked a lot about a place called 'Florenceville.' None of it made any sense. Old people often in their waning days revert back to their early childhood. Like the doctor said, probably very little of it had any basis in reality."

* *

Rev. Flowers' talk with the rest of the nursing home staff was just as unsettling. It left her not knowing what to think. Notwithstanding that the doctor said Aunt Belle's senseless ramblings were likely due to some kind of dementia, Rev. Flowers couldn't stop worrying about what her aunt had said about murder. She couldn't avoid thinking that it somehow had something to do with the missing pages in the family Bible. Something to do with the Busterson family. If Aunt Belle reverted to her childhood as the doctor believed, then perhaps she was talking about something that occurred in her childhood when the family still lived in Georgia.

Aunt Belle would have been around five or six years old then. Did she witness the murder of someone? Of someone dear to her? On the other hand, did she witness someone dear to her commit murder? The first person who came to mind was Aunt Belle's other brother, Uncle Rufus.

Uncle Rufus had a reputation in the family of always getting into trouble with the law. According to Aunt Belle, he was an embarrassment to the family. She said that when they moved to Missouri, he drifted into professional gambling and then left town. He was nothing like his big brother, Viola's grandfather Thomas Sr., who became the leading black minister in Missouri.

One story had it that a white girl with whom Uncle Rufus was romantically involved killed herself because of him. Then her bigoted father and some of his redneck friends came after him with a rope, which caused the whole family to pack up and flee the South. Although the white girl in the story committed suicide, was it really murder? Did Uncle Rufus murder that girl? Was that why the family left the South in such a hurry? What other reason was there. Nothing else made sense.

In those days in the Jim Crow South a black man killing a white woman was the most horrendous crime imaginable. If that was what happened, no wonder her grandfather changed the family name from "Busterson" to "Crombie," and ripped the family's real identity from the Bible.

Suddenly an even more chilling thought hit Viola like a rock between the eyes. Maybe Aunt Belle as a small child actually saw Uncle Rufus kill that white girl. Maybe he made her promise not to tell anyone. Did that child spend a lifetime carrying that dark secret locked inside of her? "What an awful thing!" Viola shivered.

Spent, Rev. Flowers dragged herself back to her rented car with a sodden heart. Maybe her search was turning into more than she had bargained for. Half of her wanted to drop everything and hurry home to Los Angeles. What she was unearthing was becoming just too painful. The other half of her urged her to stay and see it through, for that part of her wanted to know the truth.

On her drive back to Aunt Jennie's home, after her mind had a chance to clear up some, she concluded that maybe things weren't as bad as she was imagining. That maybe she was exaggerating things. Truthfully speaking, there was nothing concrete that Uncle

Rufus had anything to do with that white woman's death. In fact, there was nothing concrete that such a woman ever existed. It was only a story.

Putting a happier face on things made her feel better about continuing her research. However, a trip to Florenceville would have to wait until another time. For she had promised Aunt Jennie that she would spend some time with her before returning to Los Angeles.

Chapter Twenty-six

One day in Los Angeles Rev. Flower received a telephone call
from Aunt Jennie in Atlanta. "Vi, do you remember the pastor and
his wife we met at Pleasant Creek Baptist Church a couple weeks
ago? They were killed Sunday," Aunt Jennie said in a horrified
voice.

"Oh, no! What happened?" Rev. Flowers exclaimed in
disbelief, thinking it was a car accident or something.

When visiting Aunt Jennie in Atlanta Rev. Flowers wanted to
attend church services somewhere while in Georgia. She wanted a
church with plenty of good preaching and singing. There wasn't a
Church of God & Spirit in Atlanta, so she asked about a Church of
God in Christ. However, since they were short on time Aunt Jennie
took her to nearby Pleasant Creek Baptist Church instead, which
was a small church over a hundred years old with roots deep in the
black community. It was well known in Atlanta for its lively
services.

That day after church Rev. Flowers wanted to meet the
minister to congratulate him on his excellent sermon. While
waiting for the minister who was tied up with some parishioners on
church business, Aunt Jennie introduced her to the minister's wife,
a pleasant, round-faced woman who wasted no time showing Aunt
Jennie and Rev. Flowers snapshots of her beautiful grandchildren.

"Our oldest grandchild's going to Morehouse next year," she
told them with a big proud smile.

Rev. Flowers recalled how the kindly old grandmother had
bubbled with love for the children of the church as well. Small
wonder they had such a vibrant Sunday school, Rev. Flowers
thought at the time. She evaluated churches by the size of their
Sunday schools. "The larger the Sunday school, the healthier the
church," was her theory.

When Rev. Holt joined them at the door, she talked to him
briefly about his coming out to California someday and preaching
at her church. Everything was so hopeful that day. Now the Holts
were gone. God had taken them away that swiftly. It was another

instance of the old adage that tomorrow wasn't promised to anyone. She thought of Donnell Fisher, a big strapping football player from her church who had hopes of playing in the NFL someday. On the first day of practice last fall, in his senior year of high school, he suddenly dropped dead for no apparent cause. Although an autopsy was done, the cause of his death was never determined.

"It was awful, Vi! Just awful!" Aunt Jennie told her about the Holts. "Yesterday while Rev. Holt and Mrs. Holt were shaking hands with worshippers out on the steps after church, a longtime member of the church walked over and pulled out a .44 caliber pistol and shot them both in the chest. Then the woman killed herself. All three were dead by the time the police and paramedics arrived."

"Dear Jesus!" Rev. Flowers gasped upon hearing the bad news. For a split second, as if a flashbulb went off in her face, her whole world turned a blood red. Then the red vanished, allowing her to see the happy black faces of Rev. and Mrs. Holt as she saw them a couple of weeks ago.

Her stomach fisted into a hard knot, because in her mind's eye she saw her own church with the Sunday congregation pouring out after church. She saw herself on the steps of her church shaking hands and greeting people as they left the Sunday service. She saw herself joking with the children and gently pinching the fat cheeks of babies. As a minister, she believed Sunday morning on the front steps of the church was the most rewarding time of the week. That joyous moment was also the most hopeful time of the week, for everyone was filled with love, hope, and goodwill. Those good feelings from the church often spilled out into the neighborhood, making it brighter and cheerier. Sundays were the glue that kept many families together. That kept many communities together. Therefore, for Rev. Flowers those Sunday killings in Atlanta were extra tragic. It could have been her and Albert out there on those church steps, rather than Rev. and Mrs. Holt.

Aunt Jennie filled in the details. "Other churchgoers were leaving the church at the time. When the shooting started, everybody thought the church were being attack by a street gang. Everyone started running and screaming, knocking each other down in their haste to take cover. Some ran back into the church and took refuge there. Parents made a beeline to their children who had rushed outside to play the moment services were over. Then the news quickly spread across the church grounds that the 'nutty' lady had killed the pastor and his wife," Aunt Jennie said.

"Nutty lady?" Rev. Flower asked.

"Yes. The distraught woman who did the shooting was a longtime parishioner who attended church every Sunday. She was known to be a bit unstable. Other members of the church said she talked to herself a lot. Some churchgoers said she seemed especially agitated that morning. She had no criminal history, and no record of mental illness or drug use. Nor was she a known troublemaker. The woman's father said he talked to his daughter that morning just before she went to church, and she seemed fine then."

Aunt Jennie then said with a tsk-tsk sound of revulsion, "She had to be crazy, Vi. Who else would get up on a lovely Sunday morning to go to church to kill people?"

The news disturbed Rev. Flowers greatly. She hadn't seen her job as being dangerous before. Now she wasn't sure. As a clergywoman, she came in contact with weird-acting people on a daily basis. She thought of all the homeless who came to her church every day for meals, many mumbling to themselves, often angrily, about invisible things. She knew that many of them functioned fine as long as they took their medicine, but with recent cutbacks in government funding for the poor, many of them were no longer getting their medications. Were her "nutty" people capable of coming into the dining hall of the church someday and shooting the place up? This was a question she hadn't had to ask herself before. She shuddered when she recalled how some state legislatures were making it easier for people to obtain guns, even assault weapons.

When looking down from the pulpit on Sundays, she could see the dour faces of troubled congregants. Many of her church members were people who constantly worried about losing their jobs or about not having enough money to buy food or pay their mortgage or rent. Many were people with serious illness in their family. Many were people with nagging notions of suicide in their heads. Many were tired and angry from having to work two and three jobs just to make ends meet. Many worried about their children's joining street gangs or being beaten up or shot by the police. Many had families that had unraveled or were unraveling. Yet she never feared any of them.

"Well I'm not going to start being afraid now," she counseled herself severely, "What happened at Pleasant Creek Baptist Church was an aberration. Just as a speeding semi-truck that loses control and kills a carload of innocent people is an aberration."

That evening Rev. Flowers spent nearly an hour on her knees praying for the mentally ill. She also prayed that the federal government do something about restricting guns.

Chapter Twenty-seven

Her plane roared eastwardly above dark ominous clouds. Rev. Flowers was on her way back to Georgia. This time Columbus, Georgia, where she would be staying with friends while there. She had taken advantage of an opening in her busy schedule to return to Georgia to finish her family research. It felt good to get away from Los Angeles for a few days.

The airline attendant announced on the squawk box that they were entering choppy weather and for them to fasten their seat belts. Rev. Flowers fastened hers.

Lettie wanted to come with her, since the news about Aunt Belle's prattling about a murder in the family (which wasn't exactly what Viola told her, but was how Lettie saw it nonetheless) had gotten her all worked up. Like an excited hound that had picked up the scent, Lettie felt they were onto something big. Something gruesome. Perhaps murder.

Viola offered her opinion that, if in fact there had been a murder in their family, then it was probably the white woman that Uncle Rufus had supposedly impregnated. Lettie's speculation was that it might be far worse than that, and that in her opinion, not only had their great uncle killed the white woman as rumored, but that six-year-old Aunt Belle had witnessed the murder. On her mental TV screen, Lettie saw blood spattered all over the place. She envisioned little Belle watching her own brother brutally killing someone. The killing was probably very gruesome, she speculated, because after nearly ninety years, Aunt Belle was still tormented by those memories.

"Aunt Belle must have been horrified by all that brutality," Lettie groaned, speaking like she had witnessed it herself.

However, Lettie couldn't to go to Georgia with her sister, because she didn't have any more vacation time or sick days left on her job. Her boss had warned her about all the time she had already taken off during the year. So she instructed Viola on how to search the county records, suggesting that she begin with the Georgia Historical Society. She even bought her a how-to book.

Then she added darkly, "With this new information about Aunt Belle, it's very important that you also check the morgue of the local newspaper. Check for murders around 1910."

Viola wrote it all down. It was her wont to be very fastidious about the details of things. "The devil loves working with the details," she would say, her religious version of that old chestnut about the devil being in the details.

When she landed in Columbus, Rev. Flowers rented a car at the airport and drove to her friend's home in Columbus where she would be staying. After a nice dinner, her friend's husband went out and bought a local map to help her find her way around tomorrow when she drove down to Florenceville to search the county records. Because she was but a child when there last, all Rev. Flowers could remember was that Florenceville was in or close to Dougherty County.

"Are you sure it's Florenceville, and not Florence? There's a small town north of here called Florence," her friend's husband said with a puzzled look when he couldn't find any place on the map called Florenceville.

Aunt Belle lived in the Atlanta area in the latter part of her life, but the family homestead where she spent most of her earlier years was a little town near Albany, Georgia, called Florenceville, or which Rev. Flowers thought was named Florenceville. As she remembered the town, it had a population of only a few thousand people, mostly farmers, and was located at the junction of the Savannah Western and the Central Georgia Railroads.

"I'm sure it's Florenceville. I remember its being near Albany. When I was little I used to visit my Aunt Belle who lived there, and she often took me into town with her. I remember the train junction," Viola told her friends in Columbus, recalling that Aunt Belle lived on the outskirts of Florenceville.

When a small girl she loved going down South with her father to visit Aunt Belle in Florenceville, Georgia. She remembered Aunt Belle's old wood-burning cooking stove in the kitchen that always had something boiling on top or something delicious baking in the oven. She remembered the nutmeg grater that Aunt Belle kept hanging beside the stove to spice up the pies and puddings that she was always making. Aunt Belle loved to cook.

Viola remembered the times when she went hiking with Aunt

Belle along the dirt roads and railroad tracks looking for wild berries. On one such hiking trip Aunt Belle suddenly stopped and took little Viola by the arm and carefully guided her away from a promising looking patch of berries. "Don't go in those bushy weeds, child. There're probably snakes in there." She pointed to some dragonflies flying amid the dewberries. "Down here in Georgia these dragonflies are called 'snake doctors' because snakes eat them for medicine," she told little Viola, frightening her so much that she didn't want to pick any more wild fruit and berries.

Little Viola enjoyed listening to Aunt Belle talk about her father when he was a small boy. "That boy was always getting into mischief. Tom was very strict on your father, sometimes a little too strict. He was deathly afraid that Little Tom would get into trouble with the law. The law was very hard on black folks in those days, especially the males," Aunt Belle explained.

The "Tom" Aunt Belle was talking about was her big brother (Vi and Lettie's grandfather) before he became an important bishop of his church. "Little Tom" was her nephew, Vi and Lettie's father.

Talking about the law always seemed to make Aunt Belle very nervous, Viola recalled. This was quite strange since Aunt Belle wasn't afraid of white people.

Vi remembered the time when she once went shopping in Florenceville with Aunt Belle. It was the day when Aunt Belle excoriated a white teenage clerk in a drugstore they had entered to buy ice-cream cones. After requiring them to wait until all the white children were served first, even those who came into the drugstore after them, the young white female clerk finally began serving them their ice-cream. While scooping the ice-cream she looked up and saw little Viola hugging a rag doll she had taken down from the rack.

"Put that down! I should make you buy it now! Nobody'll want that doll now that you've had your black hands on it!" the young clerk screamed at little Viola, causing her to cry.

Aunt Belle was furious. Her eyes blazing, her index finger wagging, she exclaimed to the young white clerk, "You apologize to that child for screaming at her like that, or else I'll come behind that counter and teach you a lesson you'll never forget!" The white teenager's eyes inflated like balloons. She had never been spoken to like that before by a black person. Other white customers had now entered the drugstore and looked on in disbelief.

"I said apologize!" Aunt Belle demanded as she moved to go around the counter.

Terrified, the young clerk looked at Aunt Belle, then at the other white people watching to see what she was going to do. Then she broke into tears and fled to the office in the back.

The owner rushed out to see what had happened, but when he saw who the angry black woman was, his fleshy white face relaxed. Aunt Belle, a nurse, was a longtime customer who over the years had sent him many of her patients with their prescriptions.

"Is something wrong, Belle?" he asked her politely.

"You should teach your employees how to treat your customers properly," she upbraided him for what had just happened.

He apologized profusely for his young clerk, explaining that she was a new employee. He offered little Viola the doll as a gift from the store.

The child gladly took it.

"No. I'll pay for it, Mr. Finley," Aunt Belle insisted, referring to the doll. She opened her big black pocketbook and handed him some money. "And don't forget to take out for our ice-cream cones," she added. After receiving her change, she twirled on her heels, took little Viola by the hand, and left the drug store.

Now years later Viola was certain the town where they went for ice-cream that day was named Florenceville. She checked the map herself, but she too couldn't find a Florenceville anywhere.

She recalled that the town had a bustling main street and a busy county hall. Finding no such town on the map, she started having doubts that she had remembered things correctly.

"Maybe Florenceville's too small to be on the map," her friend ventured a possibility. They decided not to worry about it, and adjourned to the living room where they chatted about old times till nearly midnight.

The next morning, bright and early, Rev. Flowers took off in her rented car for Dougherty County to find the Town of Florenceville. She saw why her friend had called Dougherty County the pecan capital of the world. She hadn't seen so many pecan trees in her life.

When in Dougherty County she stopped at several truck stops

to inquire about the whereabouts of Florenceville, and even the veteran truckers hadn't heard of the town. "Is it a section of Albany?" one white trucker at one truck stop asked, thinking it might be a colored section of town that he hadn't heard of.

Finally an old man at another coffee shop told her, "There used to be a little village south of here years ago called Florenceville. It's gone now," he told her.

Viola figured that if the Town of Florenceville had been taken over by Dougherty County, then Dougherty County would have those old records. Since Albany was the seat of Dougherty County, she drove there. She first checked the county court records, the tax records, and even at the coroner's office. She found nothing. She next checked the city records and found nothing there either.

A black woman at the front desk at city hall eyed Rev. Flowers' disappointed face, and asked her if she needed help. Rev. Flowers told her about the work she and her sister were doing on their family tree, omitting, of course, the part about a possible murder in the family many years ago.

The woman's eyes blossomed like tulips when she learned that Rev. Flowers was searching her roots. "You and your sister should be congratulated. I believe more black people should know about their roots. More of us should know where our families came from," she told Rev. Flowers. She asked Rev. Flowers if she had read Alex Haley's book, *Roots,* and Rev. Flowers said she had. They then talked awhile about the Root's TV miniseries that ran some years ago.

"That was when I first became interested in doing our family history," the woman told the nice lady minister from L.A.

She tried to help Rev. Flowers get unstuck. "If there's one place in town that would have information on black folks, it would be the *Southern Freedom Star*. The Star's been reporting on black folks in this part of Georgia for over a hundred years now. Most black people around here read it religiously to see if they're in it. They have very good church news," she said, then adding, "When my young nephew drowned a few years ago, the family didn't have a picture of him, so we went to the *Star* and they had one of him at a church wedding."

Before turning to leave, she gave Rev. Flowers directions to the Southern Freedom Star building. "If you need any more help while in Albany, please don't hesitate to call me." She wrote down and handed Rev. Flowers her name and telephone number.

The *Southern Freedom Star* was a small African American weekly newspaper in the black section of town. In most American towns and cities years ago, black people depended on their black newspapers for their Negro news. Albany was no exception. In those days, except for crime, white newspapers essentially ignored the affairs of black people. The black community believed that white newspapers covered black crime because such news justified keeping black people racially segregated. The white press seemed interested only in news that showed blacks to be dumb, lazy, immoral, or lawless. Therefore, in those days, and many people say even today, the black community needed the black press for the positive news on black achievements necessary for black pride. This also included black sports news because back then the white media ignored black athletes in the belief they didn't count. This was before the days of television and national ads.

Moreover, back then black people needed the black classified ads to find the jobs and housing available to them as Negroes. In other words, back in those days, most of the vital information that black people needed for their survival was available only in Negro newspapers. Today, most of those black newspapers around the country were gone; certainly few were still flourishing like the *Southern Freedom Star*.

The *Star* was founded in 1905 by Jim Hardy as an sixteen-page Negro weekly that in the beginning he sold himself each week on the street corners of the Negro community. The newspaper grew rapidly in circulation and staff, and in short order became a race fighter worthy of the sobriquet. It always led the way on civil rights, going way back, whether fighting lynchings or police brutality. In fact, Jim Hardy testified before US Congress in Washington, DC when the NAACP pushed for federal anti-lynching legislation after World War One. At the time Negro farmers claimed that the Ku Klux Klan had undertaken a reign of terror to drive them off their farm land. But the Dixiecrats blocked the anti-lynching bills in committee.

Starting with only sixteen pages, the newspaper was now at least sixty-four pages every week.

Old Mr. Hardy loved his people—black people. He believed

Booker T. Washington and Dr. W.E.B. Du Bois were both right. He believed the Negro race needed both skilled craftsmen and learned scholars to break free from the fetters of Jim Crowism. His newspaper always respected the native intelligence of black folks, which he believed was quite high.

"You don't survive all we have been through without being very intelligent," he would say about black folks. He once wrote: "My old friend Ida B. Wells of the *Memphis Evening Star* tells her reporters to never use a word of two syllables where one syllable would do. I understand her point, but I want my readers to reach higher than that. I tell my reporters to use as many syllables as they please, so long as the context of the story is understandable to the common guy on the street. I want our readers to stretch their minds as well as receive information."

The Hardy family was able to do with the *Southern Freedom Star* something most African American businesses were unable to do: successfully pass the business down from generation to generation, with each succeeding generation improving and growing the business. Now in its fourth generation, the *Star* was as good a newspaper as any weekly in the country. The newspaper was now run by a great grandson. Unlike many black newspapers that became ancient relics in their communities, the Hardy family had succeeded in keeping the *Southern Freedom Star* modern, vibrant and relevant.

The newspaper was housed in a neatly kept brick building next door to a drug store. After hearing what she was looking for, the receptionist took Rev. Flowers back to a large room that she said was their morgue. The room was lined with filing cabinets and high metal shelves loaded with labeled boxes of old archived editions of the newspapers. Everything was neat and orderly. There was a well-lit library table in the center of the room, with some chairs for reporters doing their research. There were computers on desks spaced around the room.

The receptionist gave Rev. Flowers a few cursory instructions on how to find things and left. As Viola Flowers stood there alone unsure about where to begin, a young bespectacled man walked in and asked, "May I help you?" At first she thought he was a cub reporter, but after he introduced himself, she recognized the name. James Hardy the III was the young publisher and editor-in-chief of the paper. He was the great grandson of the founder. While his great grandfather started out in life as a common laborer, James Hardy the III graduated with honors from the University of Chicago.

Since Rev. Flowers was the granddaughter of a great man who had likewise started from humble beginnings and then founded an important institution, she felt a close kinship with young James Hardy. Both of their families stood for family legacy, important things in the black community.

She told young Hardy, "I'm researching my family roots. I'm Rev. Flowers from the Church of God & Spirit in Los Angeles. My family came from around here someplace. I think a place called Florenceville."

He scratched his smooth unwhiskered chin as he pondered how to best advise her on how to start her search. "Is Flowers your family name?" he asked, walking toward a cabinet of index cards.

"No. It's Crombie," she replied nervously, her heart pounding. The instant the name "Crombie" left her lips, her body stiffened. It was like turning a key in the door of a mysterious room and fearing what was on the other side.

He fingered through the index cards. "Next month we plan to start putting all this stuff on computer. All the digitizing equipment has been ordered," he told her, making light conversation as he flipped through the cards.

"Nothing on Crombie," he reported after going through all the cards. Seeing the disappointment on her face, he asked, "When did your family live here?" He wanted to narrow the time scope of her search.

"Around 1910," she told him with bated breath.

Because she trusted him, she came dangerously close to telling him about Aunt Belle and a possible murder around that time. However, realizing that her family's reputation was at stake, she caught herself in the nick of time. She thought of her grandfather, the Bishop T. J. Crombie, who although dead was still an icon in the gospel world. She thought of her father, also dead now, who too had been a bishop of their church. So she decided it was best to keep the murder angle to herself, for after all young Hardy was a reporter, and probably a very good one.

The young man walked over to the racked boxes and took

down a box marked "1910." He placed it on the table and told her, "Go through these, Rev. Flowers. If you don't find what you're looking for, come and get me, and I'll take down some more boxes for you. Also it might be on microfilm."

He left her alone to do her research.

Rev. Flowers didn't have to search long. Right there, near the top, inside the 1910 box was the edition of the newspaper she was looking for. It was lying there like a tarantula waiting to strike. When she reached into the box, it bit her. The headline screamed out loudly: LOCAL NEGRO PREACHER WANTED FOR MURDERING WIFE.

"Oh dear Jesus!" she gulped when she read that a local minister named Thomas Busterson had murdered his young wife. Rev. Flowers' head started spinning like a roulette wheel. She felt faint. Her chair felt like it was teetering on a high wire, so she grabbed the table to keep from falling off. She hung on for dear life for what seemed like an eternity.

Gradually her head stopped spinning and her stomach settled down. Realizing where she was, she sat up straight in her chair, composed herself, and looked around to see if anyone had seen her sobbing. She gave a big sigh of relief that she was still alone in the room. She strove to be strong. "Compose yourself, Viola! There's nothing here that says that this Rev. Busterson was grandpa." With wet eyes, she read more of the article.

The news story rehashed the grim details of the murders, stating that the murder victims were found in bed naked and their bodies blasted to pieces by shotgun fire. The newspaper article also discussed the two-month investigation that followed and how many suspects had been questioned over the course of the investigation.

"What really broke this case open was the little prayer book we found that belonged to the deceased female," the sheriff said in the article. What he didn't tell the press, however, was that his deputy found the small calf-hided prayer book when he first arrived at the scene of the murders. Thinking it would make a nice gift for his wife, he took it without telling the sheriff about it. To the deputy, the crime was only the murder of two niggers, which wasn't considered important in those parts. Then a month or so later when he realized that the sheriff was investigating the murders in earnest, he finally confessed and turned the prayer book over to the sheriff, and took his tongue-lashing like a man for taking that important piece of evidence. From the prayer book the sheriff was able to make the identification of the dead woman. Once her identity was known, he knew what direction to take the investigation. A shotgun that some fishermen retrieved from the river also helped considerably.

The sheriff was quoted as saying: "After a two-month investigation, I now have proof that Rev. Busterson murdered those two people in the cabin. He resigned from his church two months ago, and moved his family North. We have a warrant out for his arrest. He can't get away. We will get him. I promise you that." The Sheriff then described the murder suspect's family as an ailing widowed mother and two younger siblings.

Was the old ailing mother her great grandmother? Rev. Flowers wondered. Were the two siblings her great Uncle Rufus and Aunt Belle?

Hands trembling, she put the newspaper down again; she just couldn't read anymore. That the murder fugitive might have been her beloved grandfather was almost more than she could handle. She buried her face in her hands and cried like a baby.

"Dear God, what shall I tell Lettie!" she moaned wretchedly.

****

Needing to think about what to do next, Rev. Flowers went to a nearby coffee shop and had a cup of coffee. She needed it. She was trembling like someone just pulled from a bad automobile wreck. She cursed the day when Lettie brought that so-called family Bible to Los Angeles.

Tears filled her eyes again. In her muddled mind, she saw the imaginary headlines in newspapers around the country: "Founder of Black National Church A Murderer." Because the story had blood, gore, sex, and an iconic religious figure, even the white press would cover the story. She shuddered when she imagined TV shows like 60 Minutes and Dateline scouring every nook and cranny in Albany, Georgia, digging up dirt on her grandfather. She could see her father being dragged into the story somehow. After all, he too was a well-known clergyman in gospel circles. She could see herself being a part of the story. As plain as day, she could see all the reporters with their TV vans parked in front of her church in Los Angeles waiting for her to come out and appear before their cameras. She shuddered when she thought of the unsuspecting officers at the Church of God & Spirit's national headquarters in St. Louis being blindsided by news-hungry white reporters asking questions about a matter that the national church officials knew nothing about. How could they know. It all happened before the Church of God & Spirit existed.

"Calm down, Viola," she admonished herself, "There's no proof that this Rev. Thomas Busterson was grandpa. There's no proof that this is the same Busterson family that's in the family Bible. It might be just a coincidence. Most of all, there's no proof that Rev. Busterson, whoever he was, actually committed those murders. According to the newspaper articles, that was only the conclusion of one person, the sheriff. Arresting officers have been wrong before. There had been no trial or jury determination. Isn't a person presumed innocent until proven guilty?" she asked herself.

On the other hand, she had to admit that it didn't look good. Not good at all. There was material on a family named Busterson ripped from their family Bible. That was a fact. What's more, the newspaper articles said that the murder fugitive escaped from the area with his widowed mother and two younger siblings. Her Great Grandmother Lillie, her Great Uncle Rufus, and her Great Aunt Belle matched that description perfectly. That was a fact. She had heard from Aunt Belle's own lips that Grandma Lillie was in poor health when the family moved to Missouri. Was that a coincidence as well?

"Should I investigate further, or should I call the search off and go home?" she asked herself painfully. If she went farther, there might not be any turning back. "I must call Lettie and see what she thinks. This involves her too," she whimpered.

Rev. Flower got up from the booth and drove back to Columbus where she was staying.

Chapter Twenty-eight

Fortunately, that night when she got back to her friend's home in Columbus, her hosts were out running errands, which gave her the privacy in the house she needed to call her sister in Los Angeles. She reached Lettie just as she was getting home from work.

"Oh my God! Oh my God!" was all Lettie could say, over and over like a broken record, as she listened to Viola's grim tale over the telephone.

"Tomorrow I'll go back to Albany and talk to Mr. Hardy at the *Southern Freedom Star*. He was very nice. He'll know how to investigate this matter. What do you think?"

Lettie nearly went bananas, "No! Vi—are you crazy! He's a reporter! He's the last person you should talk to about this!" She could see their lives being dragged through the mud. She felt that Viola was too frank and honest to handle such a messy situation. She believed that great discretion would be required. "Maybe you should come right home, Vi, and I'll fly to Albany next week and get to the bottom of this," she said in a manner that sounded like an order.

"Are you suggesting I'm incapable of handling this?" Viola snapped back at being treated like a child. She deeply resented Lettie's didactic tone of voice.

"Vi, I only meant that this situation's very delicate. No one must know what it is that you're investigating. Not even your friends in Columbus. And especially not that guy at the newspaper," Lettie, having no desire to tangle with her big sister even from that great distance, said in a lighter tone.

Then she said, "I suggest, Vi, that you go back to that nice lady at city hall tomorrow and see if she'll help you find somebody in Albany who might've been around in 1910. There still might be somebody around who remembers the Bustersons. Old black people down there live a surprisingly long time. And they are good at remembering things a long time ago. Be careful, though. Keep it general. Don't tell anyone specifically what you're looking for.

People are quick at putting two and two together."

"That's a good idea. The lady at city hall seemed eager to help me. She's the person in her family who's doing their family tree."

Hearing a car pull into the driveway, Viola hesitated mid-sentence, looked out the window, and then said, "I must get off the phone now. Dorothy and Harold are back. I'll call you tomorrow when I get back from Albany. I love you. Bye."

****

The following morning Rev. Flowers returned to Albany and made a beeline to city hall. The black woman who worked in the mayor's office agreed to have coffee with her, and recommended that they meet at a doughnut shop around the corner from city hall. Her name was Mrs. Vera Johnson.

"I'm sorry I'm a few minutes late, Rev. Flowers," she apologized as she rushed to Rev. Flowers' booth in the doughnut shop. "I had to attend a last-minute meeting."

Realizing Mrs. Johnson was on her break and had to get back to work in a few minutes, Rev. Flowers got quickly to the point, careful to steer clear of the murders.

"I'd be glad to help you, Rev. Flowers. Knowing our family roots is very important for us black folks. It's our history. It seems like my family's been living around here forever. We can trace our roots back to the days of slavery."

Against her better judgment, she had a glazed doughnut with her coffee.

Mrs. Johnson explained the difference between a family tree and the family history. "For instance, on our family history I've written five pages on Uncle Simon alone," she told Rev. Flowers, "He's my great, great, great uncle who was killed in 1868 when after the Emancipation he tried to organize a Republican Party rally for black folks in Camilla, Georgia."

She looked up at the clock nervously, then said, "At the time Uncle Simon was a candidate for Congress in that district, and had planned to address the meeting that day. Accompanied by Negro musicians in a horse and wagon who played music along the way, nearly three hundred ex-slaves from the plantations walked in a group from Albany to the affair in Camilla. The trek was festive and peaceful. A couple of miles from Camilla they were stopped by the white sheriff of Mitchell County who was intent on stopping the Negroes from entering the town to attend the rally. While my uncle and other black leaders were trying to explain to the sheriff that their intentions were peaceable, a drunken white man in the posse fired his gun at the blacks, killing my uncle. Then a gun fight broke out between the black Republicans and the white sheriff and his men. Nine blacks were killed and thirty wounded. More would have been killed had the black group not fled into the woods."

She said with pride, "That's all a part of my family history."

"That's quite some history," Rev. Flowers intoned, impressed. She was amazed at the unbelievable flip-flop of history. Today the Democratic Party was considered the political party for black people, but back in the 1860s, the Republicans, the party of Abraham Lincoln, represented the aspirations of black people.

She told Mrs. Johnson, "My research has taken me back to 1910 and a small town near here called Florenceville. My late aunt said our family came from there. I checked all the public records but could find nothing on my family, and no one knows anything about Florenceville. It's like I've hit a blank wall."

"Florenceville wasn't a town. It was an unincorporated village. That section of the county is no longer known as Florenceville. I had relatives who lived there years ago. What's your family's name?" Mrs. Johnson asked.

"Crombie," Rev. Flowers said with trepidation. That morning before leaving Columbus, she decided to try to get information on the Busterson family on the q.t., while ostensibly researching the Crombies, which meant she had to be very discreet.

Mrs. Johnson thought awhile. "I can't placed that name." Then her eyes glistened. "If your folks were from around here, Uncle Ben would know them. He knows all the black families around here, going almost back to slavery days."

"Uncle Ben?"

"Old Mr. Ben Slaughter. He's not my uncle. Everybody calls him that. He's nearly a hundred years old, but still gets around like a man half his age. His mind's as sharp as a tack. If anyone knows the old-timers in this town, it would be him. If you come back at five when I get off work, I'll drive you out to his place," Mrs. Johnson offered generously.

"That's very kind of you, Mrs. Johnson, but you needn't bother. I have a car. If you'd give me the address, I can find it."

"It's a little hard to locate." She pulled out a pen and some paper. "He lives down by the river. I'll draw you a map to help you get there. I'll call him and tell him to expect you. He's a little hard of hearing, so you must be patient with him."

Chapter Twenty-nine

Old Mr. Ben Slaughter lived in a little house near the river. Rev. Flowers was rather surprised when she first saw him. On the way to his place she imagined a white-haired, dignified, chocolate-colored gentleman who looked like the Uncle Ben on the rice box. This Uncle Ben, however, was a coal black, bent-over, wizened old man so slightly built that a strong gust of wind could blow him away.

When Rev. Flowers pulled into his driveway, he was sitting on his front porch with his dog. When Rev. Flowers got out of her car, he got up and shuffled on his cane to the edge of the porch. The dog came with him barking.

"Good morning. Are you Mr. Slaughter? I'm Rev. Viola Flowers from Los Angeles. Did Mrs. Vera Johnson call you that I was coming?"

From the look on his thin black face, she could see he was puzzled why she was there in his yard.

"Vera Johnson? Sadie Johnson's little girl?"

Rev. Flowers nodded in the affirmative and approached the porch. She assumed that Sadie Johnson's little girl was that fortyish-something woman at city hall who had told her about him. She introduced herself again.

"I see you're a fisherman," she smiled, her eyes pointing to the fishing poles and tackle box on the porch.

"I was out early this morning and caught a few nice size bass. When I was younger I used to take my boat out. Now I have to fish from the river bank. When you're an old man my age, there ain't much else you can do," he gummed, smiling.

What he didn't tell her was that a few years ago his daughter and son-in-law took his rowboat away from him after he went out on the river one day to fish and got lost. Some white fishermen found him drifting down the river petrified. Although he was only a few hundred feet off shore, he had lost his bearings and panicked. It was his old age. He had been boating that river safely for over eighty year, and he knew it like the back of his hand. Then his mind failed him. Fortunately his fishing line snagged on something that kept him from going down the river and drifting into the Gulf of Mexico. Now his children had restricted him to the river bank.

Mr. Slaughter and Rev. Flowers elected to sit out on the porch and talk. He shuffled into the house and like a proper Southern gentleman brought her out a cool glass of water. They talked awhile about fishing. Then his mind flew off like an escaped canary, and he began talking about the big flood of 1932 when all the homes in the area were washed away. Vera Johnson had warned her that he would sometimes drift off in the middle of a sentence like he had been suddenly transported back in time. "Just bear with him. He'll eventually get back to you," Mrs. Johnson told her.

"Who's your kin, child?" he finally got around to asking as he lit up his pipe.

"The Crombies. Sam and Lillian," she told him, careful not to reveal too much about her family. If possible, the object of her mission was to get information on the Bustersons without staining the good name of her family. She waited anxiously for his reply.

His brow knotted in thought as his old mind plowed backward in time through all the memories cluttered there. His mind was like an old jalopy backing up in mud, and Rev. Flowers could almost hear the wheels groaning. Then his face sprung alive like a blooming sunflower. The tires of his memory had gotten some traction. "You mean the Crombies who used to live over on Brier Street? A nice family. Years ago Bud Crombie and I played together in a riverboat band. Bud was the best musician to come from these parts. He played trombone. He ended up going up to Chicago. All those Crombies are dead now. Were they kinfolks of yours?"

"No, I don't think so," she said with uncertainty as she wondered where those Crombies came from. She didn't find anything on them in the public records. She wondered if Bud Crombie was black. If so, was she related to him? Did she and Lettie still have paternal relatives in the Deep South that they didn't know about? She made a mental note to check that out later.

Her heart in her mouth, she asked the old man fearfully, "Did those Crombies have sons named Thomas and Rufus and a daughter named Belle?"

The old man took his time. His mind clonked back in time again. This time he must have made a pit stop somewhere along the way, for he just sat there silently for a long spell looking serene. The memory must have been pleasant because he had the pleased look of a cat that had just eaten.

He blinked and said, "I don't remember any family around here with a son named Rufus. Then his brow crinkled and his eyes narrowed, for he had remembered something. The sunflower face reappeared. "D'you mean Rufus Busterson? He's the only Rufus I can recall who lived around here. That boy was hell on wheels!"

Rev. Flowers stiffened and her eyes widened.

Mr. Slaughter's old face darkened again, "Rufus was always getting into trouble. He loved to fight. I remember once when he pulled a plank off Mrs. Rogers' picket fence and hit the Macfall boy in the head with it. He put that poor boy in the hospital. Rufus Busterson was a bad egg." Old Uncle Ben was now scowling like someone with acute indigestion. He was now remembering other things about the Bustersons that apparently were leaving a bad taste in his mouth.

Rev. Flowers was so stunned by that last bit of information that she almost fell off her chair. The old man had just described Uncle Rufus to a T, at least the Uncle Rufus that Aunt Belle had told her about.

Old Man Slaughter sucked his gums as old folks were wont to do. "Now the older Busterson boy was just the opposite. He was the good one. He was hardworking, dependable and deeply religious. In fact he became a preacher, and a good preacher, too. Could that young man preach!"

Mr. Slaughter's face brightened; then just as quickly it saddened. "No telling how far he would've gone if not for that hot-tailed wife of his."

"Wife?" Rev. Flowers' eyes bulged larger. It was news to her that her grandfather had another wife back then. She had always assumed that Grandma Dolly was his first and only wife.

The old man put another match to his pipe and got it going again, making a loud gurgling sound. "Yep. You remember that Higgins girl from Atlanta he married, don't you?" he said, talking to Rev. Flower like she had grown up around there. "That hot-tailed girl chased boys around the church like a little bitch in heat.

I'm sorry to use language like that, young lady, but you know yourself that what I'm saying is true. We all knew he shouldn't have married that girl. She was no proper wife for a minister. She was too fast and wild to be a preacher's wife. People tried to talk to him about her, but he wouldn't listen to anybody. He loved her too much."

Mr. Slaughter shook his old wrinkled head in disgust, "There's nothing as stupid as a man in love. And sure enough, that little she-devil ended up getting that good Christian man into a heap of trouble."

"In trouble?" Rev. Flowers gasped again.

"Yes Ma'am. Little Miss swishy-tail got herself killed. Somebody blew her brains out. She was found dead, naked in a cabin out in the woods. Somebody walked in and killed her and her lover. Some folks around here believed Rev. Busterson was innocent, but most of us knew he did it. That he was driven to it. That he had no choice. He caught them in bed together and shot them. She asked for it. She would brazenly flirt with men right in front of him, and he would pretend he didn't see it. She would throw her dirty affairs in his face, rub them in, and then laugh at him. That poor man. We all thought she got what she deserved. Even the sheriff thought so. For a long time he didn't make an arrest. We think he deliberately gave Rev. Busterson time to pack up his family and get out of town. You remember that, don't you? The whole town was talking about it."

The old man still saw Rev. Flowers as a townsperson with whom he was gossiping about the town's most infamous crime.

Rev. Flowers got to her feet. She was dumbfounded by what she had heard. She had heard enough. She glanced at her watch. "My, how time flies. I hadn't realized it was so late. I must go now. Thank you, Mr. Slaughter, for giving me the time. You were very helpful," she told him, making an excuse so she could leave.

She had gotten the information she wanted, and wanted to leave before he connected her to the Busterson scandal. To seek more would be dangerously pushing it, she figured. He had forgotten about her family-tree question. In fact he had forgotten that she was the lady from California researching her family history.

"I thought you were staying for lunch, Margaret," he said as he got up with disappointment on his old face. "I'd planned to fry us up a delicious mess of that bass I caught this morning. I was hoping you'd take some home to your mama and the kids."

Now he had confused Rev. Flowers with someone named Margaret.

"Maybe next time, Mr. Slaughter. Thank you anyway."

"Goodbye." She shook his hand and quickly departed.

A block or so from his house, she pulled her car over and threw up.

Chapter Thirty

The trip home to Los Angeles was the longest plane ride of Rev. Flowers' life. What she learned in Albany had left her reeling like a drunk and she needed to get home. She thought of her sister and grimaced, for she wasn't looking forward to telling Lettie what old Mr. Slaughter had told her. Lettie had wanted her to call from Georgia if she discovered anything important in Albany. She knew Lettie had waited anxiously in Los Angeles for that call. And she had picked up the telephone several times to call Lettie, but each time she just couldn't go through with it.

She worried about how Lettie would take the bad news. With their family having never faced anything this grave before—anything this dark and ominous before—would Lettie go to pieces over the terrible news? Lettie was such a proud person. In fact she could be a little uppity about their family at times. She was very proud of being a Crombie, and was fond of telling people about her grandfather and father both being bishops. Of course she was very proud of her sister Viola.

Lettie was a pleasure to be with when sharing great news. And she had wonderful little spur-of-the-moment ways of celebrating good news, such as ordering as her treat Chinese food from the best restaurant around that would deliver. Or, if everyone was in the mood, she would take everybody out to a fancy restaurant for dinner to celebrate the good news. She was a very generous person, and always did things that made the occasion extra special.

For example, the year when Rev. Flowers won the "Gospel Broadcaster of the Year Award," she helped Viola and Albert celebrate the award in a grand manner, and it was all a big surprise to Rev. Flowers. With Albert's help, but unbeknownst to Viola, Lettie arranged for a stretch limousine to be waiting after the ceremonies at the Shrine Auditorium. She paid for everything from money she had saved for a vacation in Hawaii.

She had Albert secretly packed Vi's overnight things and put the suitcase in the trunk of the limousine, sans Viola's knowledge. You could have knocked Rev. Flowers over with a feather when she walked out of the theater that night still in her long evening gown and wearing a beautiful corsage, and saw this chauffeur and his long black limousine waiting for her and Albert. The block-long automobile (or so it seemed) had television and all the other elaborate furnishings. At first Viola thought such luxurious transportation home was a part of her award. Albert would tell her later that everything was at the courtesy of Lettie.

When the chauffeur opened the car door, there sat a dining table with white linen and place settings for two, complete with an elegantly dressed waiter.

"Albert, where are we going?" she asked, excited.

"You'll see," he said, "Just don't eat too much, because dinner's waiting for us where we're going." He was referring to the hors d'oeuvres. Then the waiter cracked open the champagne.

When the limousine pulled off, Viola waved to her adoring supporters standing on the sidewalk, who wildly waved back. Lettie was also out there on the sidewalk pointing out proudly to the other onlookers that Rev. Flowers was her sister.

The limousine then took them to a five-star seafood restaurant high on a cliff overlooking the Pacific Ocean, all paid for by Lettie.

However, Lettie could be a big pain in the ass when the news was bad. While Albert was always a comfort in times of trouble, in difficult times Lettie usually made matters worse. For example, initially Lettie was unconcerned about the torn-out pages in the old Bible. She offered a hundred different explanations why those missing pages were unimportant. She believed there was nothing to worry about. First she postulated that Aunt Belle had probably given Aunt Jennie the wrong Bible by mistake due to old age.

"Who knows? You know how some old people are. They reach for one thing, while really wanting something else," she said glibly at the time.

Or the explanation that it was probably a hand-me-down Bible. "Maybe someone in the family got that Bible from the Salvation Army or some other secondhand store, and that stuff on the Busterson family was already in there when they got it, and had to be torn out. You know how black folks used hand-me-down things back in those days."

These were the main explanations she gave in response to her big sister's concern about the missing pages. But when she learned of Aunt Belle's delusions in the nursing home, her negative imagination caught fire and blazed like dry brushwood. To her, the delusions had to mean there had been a gruesome murder in the family. As was typical of her, she quickly dreamed up the worst scenario imaginable. "Vi, that's awful! Just awful! That our family was involved in those awful murders!" she wailed like a chicken about to have its head cut off.

Viola answered, "Lettie, I didn't say anything about our family murdering anybody. I only said that the nursing staff said that Aunt Belle often babbled about murder. That her babbling made no sense. As one of the nurses said, she might've been disturbed about something she saw recently on TV."

Lettie never married mostly because she always drove men away with her wild accusations about other women. It wasn't jealousy exactly that spoiled things for her. It was that weird brand of negativity that she sometimes had. Most negative people see only the bad in people, but Lettie wasn't like that. She could see the good in people. People liked her and she was very popular at work. Men liked her, and many had asked for her hand. It was just that it didn't take much to get her worrying about things. One might say she was a bit of a worrywart.

And when Lettie started worrying, she took it to the extreme. To her if the worst could happen, then it likely would happen. Viola believed Lettie was like that because she had no real spiritual foundation. She didn't have the faith that Viola had that fate can be confidently left in the hands of the Lord. As with many preachers' children, Lettie had rebelled against her religious upbringing early in life, and quit attending church on a regular basis when she was emancipated as a teenager. Even today Viola had trouble getting her to church.

A flight attendant ordered everyone to fasten their seat belts and Rev. Flowers fastened hers. "Is Lettie strong enough to take it?" she sighed forlornly as her plane banked to land.

Chapter Thirty-one

Rev. Flowers sat in her office with a heavy heart and stared at
her grandfather's framed photograph on her wall. His eyes seemed
to be avoiding hers. This large imposing black man who ruled his
church with an iron fist. Her hero. This moral giant that she
admired so much and after whom she had patterned much of her
life. She was very proud that back in his day he was light years
ahead of most black church leaders on the issue of women's rights.
When her grandfather was a young minister in the Church of
Christ, the Church of Christ didn't allow the ordination of women.
From the very beginning her grandfather opposed that policy and
fought to have it changed.

"Limiting the role of women in the church is a lot of nonsense.
We should be ashamed of ourselves. My mother ran our little
church and preached every Sunday for nearly twenty years before a
male minister was finally sent to our little town. So I know what
women can do, and so does God," he argued with church leaders at
every opportunity.

Then he started speaking out forcefully against the policy from
the pulpit on Sundays, and the church leadership censured him for
doing so. Some leaders tried to banish him from the church, but
failed because he had too many followers. He was simply too
strong and politically cunning. His followers in the church
multiplied. While supporting the Church of Christ's basic doctrines
of the infallibility of Scripture, the need for regeneration, and the
baptism of the Holy Ghost, he and his followers eventually cut all
ties with the Church of Christ, a holiness church preferred by many
African Americans at the time. He and his followers realized it was
just too difficult to make such a drastic change in doctrine from
within the church, so they left the Church of Christ and started
their own church that allowed the sanctification and ordination of
women. It angered Rev. Flowers that even today there were still
black churches in America that didn't allow women ministers in
their order.

"Did you do it, grandpa? Did you kill those people?" she asked the stern-faced black man in the photograph. "Tell me that you didn't do it," she begged him pathetically.

He still avoided looking at her; in fact he seemed ashamed to look at her. Her heart began to pound. Her face clouded. The muscles in her jaw tightened. Tears filled her eyes. At that moment she hated him. "You murdering hypocrite!" she screamed at him. Now the tears were streaming down her face.

"Shame on you, Viola Flowers," a little voice inside her said, reminding her that it was never proved in court that he committed that crime. The newspapers said there were many other people under suspicion for those murders. It mentioned a state senator and possible blackmail. And as his granddaughter, she had the right to hang on to that slender thread of hope, she convinced herself.

Besides, even if he did it, he had to account to God years ago. He had to go before that heavenly court and make amends. She wondered if he received God's forgiveness. She imagined the thousands of conversations that he and God probably had since that awful night in the woods. Surely by now God has judged him and rendered a verdict, she thought. That is, if he did it.

She caught herself. Who did she think she was sitting in judgment of God's judgment.

"Please, O Lord, forgive me. Whatever your judgment was I know it embodied your love and infinite wisdom." Her eyes shut, her finger entwined, at that moment she felt like she did the night she was saved when a child: that Jesus would always be there with her, holding her hand.

Then she apologized to the man in the picture frame, "I'm sorry, Grandpa. I don't know what came over me." .

She prayed some more.

Chapter Thirty-two

It was a few days before she and Lettie could really sit down
and talk. When they did talk, it went as Viola had feared. Lettie
was very upset that Viola intended to return to Georgia again to
run down leads that relatives on their grandfather's side possibly
still lived in Georgia. Lettie didn't see the point to it. She thought
the idea was stupid.

"You said yourself, Vi, that you didn't think the Crombie
family that the old man knew was related to us. You said he said
that those Crombies are all dead now. So what's the point?" Lettie
was referring to what Old Mr. Slaughter had told Viola.

"I'm not talking about the Crombies," Viola replied solemnly.

"What are you talking about, then?" Lettie now sensed even
greater danger. She made a curdled face. Her narrowed eyes
warned her big sister not to say what she knew she was about to
say, but Viola said it anyway.

"I'm talking about the Bustersons." Viola Flowers got up from
her kitchen table and walked to the window. She gazed out at her
backyard as her mind organized her arguments. What she was
about to say she had mulled around in her mind a million times
since talking to Old Man Slaughter. She had gone over the
evidence with a fine-tooth comb, debating with herself until purple
in the face what it all meant, and she was unhappy with the
conclusion she reached. But no other conclusion seemed plausible.
She and Lettie were Bustersons. It was very painful hearing that
voiced aloud.

The little gray squirrel she was watching darted up one of her
fruit trees and disappeared. She sighed to herself, "You live all
your life believing you're one thing, then you suddenly discover
that you're something else. It's very scary."

She turned from the window and looked at Lettie grimly and
said, "Although Mr. Slaughter seemed not to know anything about
our family, everything he said about the Bustersons matched our
family perfectly. He mentioned the widowed mother, and the
oldest son who was a minister."

Lettie cut her off sharply, "That proves nothing! There're plenty old black widows in the South with preacher sons."

Her eyes blazing hotly, Lettie was like an agitated jaybird whose nest was being threatened by cats. She regretted having started their family tree. She wanted to burn that damn old Bible. She thought that Viola's idea about returning to Georgia was insane. Absolutely insane! Jaybird feathers were now flying everywhere.

Although Lettie had been quick to jump to conclusions about murder from the scant information they had gotten at Aunt Belle's nursing home, she was now less quick to accept responsibility for those conclusions. Now that they had in fact found a murder, she was fighting everything Viola was proffering to explain how it all related to them.

Rev. Flowers continued with her argument, "Then there was the Busterson's youngest son named Rufus, who Mr. Slaughter said was always getting into trouble. The old man knows more about Uncle Rufus's fighting than we do."

She then said sadly, "Lettie, the thing that clinched it for me was what Mr. Slaughter said about the little Busterson girl. He said the Busterson girl—who I'm convinced was Aunt Belle—returned to Georgia some years later to live. He'd heard that from somewhere. He didn't know her name or where she lived in Georgia. He only knew that she returned."

This fact quieted Lettie somewhat. Her tear-smudged face became long and pitiful.

Now with the worse over, Viola delivered some comforting news. She could see from Lettie's sad face that she needed some solace. "There's no doubt in my mind that the Rev. Busterson in those newspaper articles is grandpa, and that we are Bustersons. I have no doubt about that. I do have doubts, however, that grandpa killed those people. Mr. Slaughter said the whole town was sharply divided on that question. He said that even the sheriff didn't want to make an arrest after he had all the facts. He said the sheriff closed the case without really looking for grandpa. He said the sheriff felt there were too many unanswered questions in the case to make the arrest."

Rev. Flowers hesitated for a moment, then said, "It seemed the young man who was murdered had a long criminal record, and that out-of-town gangsters might've killed him and his girlfriend. Mr. Slaughter said there was also some talk about an important white politician being involved. There were many theories about who committed those murders. How are we supposed to know what the truth is?"

She closed sadly, "I only hope that if grandpa did it—and I don't think he did—that God forgave him. That he found redemption."

Still not totally convinced, Lettie said, scowling, "I still think we should get rid of that damn so-called family Bible and forget about the whole damned thing. We've lived this long without knowing about our family history, so why do we need to know now."

Viola said big-sisterly, "No. We must continue the research. I don't mean that we should try to solve those awful murders. The murder investigation is closed. But we mustn't run from those murders, either. If we have skeletons in our closet, then we must get them out and give them a decent burial. The Lord's here to help us. From what Mr. Slaughter said I got the feeling that there are still some Bustersons around. If so, they are our kin. I have to go east again next month to a gospel convention in Joplin."

She got to her feet again and said, "After the convention I'll go down to Albany again and spend a few days asking questions."

"But why Vi? Why, goddamnit!" Lettie cried out hysterically. "Why drag our family through the mud when we don't have to?" To her it was stupid for them to subject themselves to such misery when they really didn't have to. Why suffer disgrace when it could be avoided.

"Not to go back to Georgia would be running from the truth," Viola argued, ignoring Lettie's profanity, "I'm too old to run from the truth. So are you. Despoiling the family name might be the price we'll have to pay for that truth, but I'm willing to pay it. We are who we are, and our family is what our family is. We must accept the bad with the good. God decrees that. We must place our faith in Him. He knows we are good people. If the Bustersons are our family, then I want to know them. The blood coursing through my veins tells me that the Bustersons are good people too. I really believe that. You should too, because the same blood flows through your veins as well."

Viola was now clearly in charge as the big sister.

Chapter Thirty-three

That night Viola and Lettie talked long into the night about Viola's returning to Georgia. Lettie begged her big sister not to, imploring her to leave the matter alone. "Why drag our family through all the scandal if we don't have to?" she beseeched, repeating a point she had been making all night long. But Viola refused to budge.

"You're so stubborn, Vi!" Lettie exclaimed, exasperated. Then she just sat there and stared at Viola like she wanted to strangle her, which Viola pretended not to notice. As it had been all their lives, it was now a battle of wills. The two women sat there for a while in silence.

Lettie relented first and was the first to break the silence. "When do you plan to leave?" she asked wanly, referring to Viola's return trip to Georgia.

"I'm attending a conference in Joplin next month. I thought after the conference I'd take a few days and go then," Viola replied, sensing that her sister was softening.

Viola looked at Lettie and said in a loving tone, "It would be nice if you could come with me."

Lettie said, "I would like to, but I don't have any vacation time left." After thinking about it for awhile, she let loose a little laugh, "What the hell—let's do it."

"Good. I'll book the tickets tonight," Viola said, getting up.

"Let's do it now," Lettie said as she fumbled in her bag for her billfold. "Here, use my credit card. You paid for the last ticket."

Viola smiled at her sister's big heartedness.

-The End-

Afterward

This is the second book in a trilogy of novels written by the author that examines strong, interesting women at home, at work, at worship, and at play, including their love lives. The third novel in this trilogy will be *The Daughters of Joe Stubbs,* a quirky but smart story about the Stubbs family. The father Joe Stubbs is content with his small law firm where making lots of money is unimportant to him. A widower and single parent, he raises his two small daughters to be very successful lawyers. Joe is very proud of them. They are a very close-knit African American family. One day Joe, a poor Southern boy in his youth, learns from a friend how much weddings cost nowadays, some exceeding $20,000. "You have two grown daughters, don't you, Joe? Well, get ready. You're probably next," the friend says. This worries Joe immensely, for he hadn't realized that weddings could be so expensive. He doesn't make that kind of money. Now for the first time in his life he begins to think of himself as a failure, both as a father and a lawyer. He goes into a humorous funk. His daughters, however, see him as their hero.

Meanwhile in the story, Joe Stubbs' oldest daughter Ollie, a deputy district attorney, has a big fight with her superiors, and threatens to resign. Her sister Risa is pleased that Ollie might resign, because maybe now they can have that family law firm she has long dreamed about that would help people, instead of just making money. A few days later, thinking Ollie wasn't home, Risa lets herself into Ollie's apartment to get something, and finds her sister Ollie in bed naked with a white woman. Risa is shocked because she had no idea that Ollie was gay. All her life Ollie has been her role model. Before storming out of Ollie's apartment in tears, Risa exclaims, "I don't care what your sexual preference is. That's your business. But when it puts down black women, that's another matter entirely. Also in tears Ollie replies, "What does my loving Jane has to do with putting down black women?"

The daughters need Joe's help to keep the family together, but he's deeply mired in gloom about his financial inability to give his daughters the great weddings he thinks they deserve. He too had no idea that Ollie was a lesbian. Can this close and loving family be put back together again?

The Daughters of Joe Stubbs will be available soon at Amazon and other bookstores where good books are sold. Pre-order now and be the first in your circle to enjoy another one of Will Gibson's gripping stories.

* *

Author WILL GIBSON founded the American Black Book Writers Association as its first president and trade journal editor-in-chief. He served on the advisory board of the Black Authors: Selection of Sketches from Contemporary Authors, Gale Research. He is the author of many novels, including *Lola & The World of Buddy Shortt* and *The Reverend Viola Flowers.*

* *

The book cover was designed by Ezekiel Sweetz, and the rights to use the photo 'Burning Book On Fire Flames' were legally acquired from Dreamtime. com.